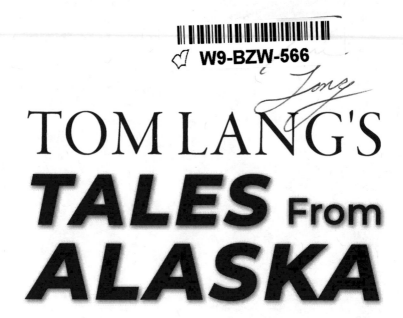
Long

TOM LANG'S
TALES From
ALASKA

Tales From Alaska
© *1995, 2018 Tom Lang All Rights Reserved*

ISBN 978096497424-1
Published by:
BOUDELANG PRESS
PO Box 852 Haines, AK 99827

WEBSITE: www.boudelang.com www.tomlangbooks.com
E-MAIL: tomlangbooks@gmail.com

Eagle © 1995, 2018
Salmon © 1998, 2018
Mrs. Claus © 1997, 2018
Bear © 2002, 2018
Moose © 2007, 2018
Wolf © 2011, 2018

Illustrations: Tim Shields
Design by Jill Sockolov
Back Cover Photo: Rustin Gooden

ISBN 978-1930124400

Praise for Tom Lang's Books

"For centuries, across the planet, the art of storytelling has been used to convey important lessons from generation to generation. More than ever, we need new tales that convey the importance and wonders of the natural world. Tommy has done just that, by engaging the reader with eloquence and humor while delivering insightful, poignant lessons. A must read for educators, kids of all ages, and all of us who love a good story."

--DR. SCOTT RAMSEY, *Director of the Alaska Outdoor Science School*

"With over twenty-five years of experience, Tom Lang has guided more guests through the Chilkat Bald Eagle Preserve than any other guide in the Chilkat Valley. His approach is always fresh and wide-eyed. Tom combines his sparkling sense of humor with his love of nature to enliven this series of small books about Alaskan wildlife. The series is a fun way to learn about the Chilkat Eagle Preserve and its most iconic inhabitants- bald eagles, moose, salmon, wolf and bear."

--JOE ORDONEZ, *Author of "Where Eagles Gather, the Story of the Alaska Chilkat Bald Eagle Preserve, Haines, Alaska."*

"I love Tom Lang's books! They make you laugh and learn at the same time. I read them to my river trip passengers and they always love them."

--CHRISTA SADLER, *International River Guide and author of "Colorado."*

"As a long time tour director in Alaska I encourage my guests to read and learn to enhance their experience in this Great Land. Tom's books are one of the best ways to do that. Enjoy!"

--RANDY HAMMOND, *Senior Tauck Director, Tauck World Discovery*

Contents

For Jayne Elizabeth Read-Lang

A Note from the Author

My mother instilled in me the love of animal mythology by reading fables to me every night when I was a young boy. She performed the voices of all the dogs, cats, wolves, bears and squirrels in the stories, pulling me deeper into the tales with her dramatic pauses and creative voice modulations. When my mother finished reading to me each night, she closed the book, brushed her hand across my head, kissed my forehead and turned off the light. I would tumble into a dream world of talking animals and thick, rich forests. When I first began guiding and giving nature talks in the Chilkat Bald Eagle Preserve in Haines, Alaska, I developed a style that revolved around explaining nature through the animal's eyes and those talks evolved into the book series that includes Eagle, Salmon, Bear, Moose and Wolf. Animal fables may be the oldest form of storytelling. They are the first Self-Help stories, moral tales spun to inspire introspection and to give life lessons for the greater good of the tribe. I've extensively studied the history of fables from Africa to Asia to Europe to South and North America and I've worked hard to create the best fables I'm capable of in my little animal books. I read every book I can find on the animal. I speak with as many of the world experts that will talk to me. I observe the creature in his habitat as much as possible, so I can merge the rhythm of his life with the rhythm of my writing. My goal for each fable is for it to be funny, educational and for the story to resonate with a timeless theme that will keep the tale relevant and thoughtful for years to come.

Welcome to Tales from Alaska and enjoy.
Tom Lang

BEAR

An Anger Management Story

I'M A BIG, BAD ALASKAN BROWN BEAR AND I GET A little angry now and then. So shoot me. I don't live in a fairy tale world where the worst thing that can happen is a smelly human eats my porridge and sleeps in my bed. I live in the real world. One day you're walking down a trail smelling the flowers, the next day your head's hanging on a cabin wall and the humans are sitting on your butt in front of the fireplace.

My last rampage started late this spring. I was eating salmon, alone as usual, along side the riverbank. A herd of cars stopped and humans got out pointing and staring at me. I moved up river but they followed me, their cameras making little insect noises. After my second salmon I snapped. I dropped the carcass and charged toward the road. The humans screamed as they raced to their cars. I banged on windows and I stood on hoods. I chewed on tires until they exploded.

"Are we having fun yet?" I growled, ripping a funny looking boat off the top of a truck and crushing it with my paws.

For the next few weeks I scared every human I could find. I shadowed campgrounds at dusk, waiting for the humans to go to sleep. Then I banged on their trailers or ripped open their tents. I sniffed along hiking trails, listening for the sound of bells and the weak squeak of the human voice. Humans always fall for the old fake charge technique. I jump out of the bushes, roaring and romping at full speed, then slam on the brakes a few feet in front of them before their smell knocks me into a coma. While the humans lie shaking, curled up in balls, I tear into their backpacks and eat their food.

Is my behavior a bit extreme? Perhaps, but I've been on edge since cubhood. I'm an insomniac. I haven't had a sound winter's sleep since I was two years old. Most brown bears catch some shuteye and hibernate for five or six months. I spend my winters lying in my six-foot-long, four-foot-wide den and staring up at my three-foot-high ceiling. I count blueberries and jumping salmon. I memorize moose anatomy. Nothing works. The few times I slip into slumber I am startled awake by my troubled dreams. At the peak of my rage this year my brother Ted came up to me as I was sneaking up on one of those humans who run for miles for no apparent reason.

"Hey, bro," he said. "I've been looking for you. Hungry?"

"I'm always hungry, Teddy."

"I have a moose hind quarter that's rotting away and I thought you and me could sit and feast on it."

"Twist my paw."

Although we live in the same valley, my brother and I don't see each other much and we haven't been close since we were cubs. But a free meal is a free meal. I followed him through the woods, making small talk: "...is it just me or are the glaciers melting faster this year... I hear there's a new parasite going around...those damn wolves."

We arrived at a clearing, a grassy moose meadow where twenty bears sat in a circle. The legendary Big Bear stood in the center while the group stared at me. Big Bear beckoned me forward with the curl of a claw. He put his big paw over my hump.

"You know everybody," Big Bear said, his voice thunder from the sky.

The bears grunted and snorted "hellos."

"What's this all about?" I said, glancing over at my brother. Teddy turned away from me and looked down at his back legs.

"This is about you," Big Bear said, first pointing at me then spreading his front legs toward the group, "and this is about us."

I nodded and waited.

"You're causing trouble with the humans," Big Bear said.

The bears in the group grumbled and huffed.

"So? They started it."

"And they'll finish it. Humans began slaughtering our forebears 200 years ago. There were 100 thousand of us down in the lower 48 ranges back then. Now there are only 1,000 left. We still have 30,000 brown bears in Alaska and we want to keep it that way. Your behavior does no one any good."

"I can't see what difference my behavior—"

Big Bear raised his paw to silence me.

"They come looking for you they come looking for all of us. Humans are stupid. We all look alike to them. They can't smell. Our sense of smell is 75 times stronger. The olfactory mucosa in a human's nose is less than a square inch. Ours is 100 times that. Humans are at the bottom of the evolutionary ladder."

"Exactly, Big Bear, so what's the problem?"

"The problem is this; by stepping down to the human's level, which you are doing by attacking for no reason, you create a problem for all of us. Humans are reactive and irrational. All they need is one lame excuse and they'll start picking us off like berries from a bush."

"What do you expect me to do about it?"

"We expect you to change your behavior. All bears have potential problems with humans. But you have a bigger problem with yourself. You're acting out. It is the summation of the Benevolent Order of Brown Bears of the Chilkat Valley that you visit Dr. Carnivora Chordata, our anger management specialist here in the valley."

"Or what?" I said, heat rising under my fur.

The group of bears stood up and surrounded me.

"Failure to do so," Big Bear said, squeezing my shoulder, "will give us no other choice but to ban you from the premier spawning grounds, restrict your roaming on Blueberry Hill and revoke your forest toilet privileges until we see fit."

I AM WALKING THROUGH THE WOODS ON A PERFECT DAY,
my nose sucking in the sweetness from the air. Spring flowers arch toward the sun,
birds play call and response and little creatures dart in and out of the brush. I
whistle a tune while the trees sway back and forth in rhythm. A wolf appears on
the trail in front of me.

"Morning, Mr. Bear, you are looking good," the wolf says. "Niiiice coat."

"Thank you, Mr. Wolf," I say.

I skip along the trail, whistling, loving life. Around the next turn a moose antler
hits me in the head.

"Hey, that's a top-of-the-line fur you got there, pal," the moose says.

"Thank you very much, Mr. Moose, only wish I had one of those things you
have hanging under your chin."

"Dewlap, Mr. Bear, it's called a dewlap."

"Whatever."

I continue on my way, bouncing and singing. A flutter of wings gives my tune a
backbeat. I look up at a bald eagle circling above the tree line.

"I thought I had beautiful feathers, but you've got one nice set of duds there, Mr. Bear."

"Thank you, Mr. Eagle," I say, saluting him with my right paw. As I step into a
creek a school of sockeye salmon jumps into the air.

"Wow," the pool of voices scream, "look at the beautiful coat, fit for the king of
the forest, which you are, of course. All hail Mr. Bear!"

"Thank you little buddies."

I stop midstream, pinched by my instincts. The forest is silent, earthquake quiet.
I look around. The wolf, moose and eagle are staring at me, smiling. The salmon
are huddled in an eddy, giggling. A streak of cold shakes me as I look down at my
paws. They're hairless. I check my legs, chest, hump. I have no coat at all, naked as
a newborn cub.

"Now, there's a bare bear," the wolf says, howling at his own joke.

The moose laughs so hard he falls down, clapping his hooves together. The eagle flaps his wings, an owl hoots from the trees, the salmon jump in and out of the water slapping their fins. The forest shakes with laughter.

I run through the woods, smashing into trees and trampling plants and flowers. I hide behind a large rock, hugging myself as I shiver in the cold, the cackles and snickers thundering in my head.

"HOW DID YOU FEEL WHEN YOUR MOTHER... UM... separated from you?"

"You mean abandoned me?"

"Okay, abandoned you. How did you feel?"

"How would you feel?"

"We're not here to talk about me, Mr. Brown."

I stood up. The sweet aroma of a distant dead moose filled me with cubhood memories of hunger and loss. I stared off into the mountains above Dr. Chordata's office.

"How old were you when your mother left?"

"Left, ha!" I huffed as I paced back and forth. "Kicked us out and ran off with a new male. We were only two-and-a-half years old. We were little cubs, barely 200 pounds."

"Eighty percent of mothers separate from their children at the start of the third summer," Dr. Chordata said, smoothing her coat with her claws.

"And that makes it right?"

I crushed an elderberry bush as I stomped to my left.

"Mr. Brown, you know the rules: no roaming. Please lay back on the skunk cabbage."

I puffed out a breath and dropped to the ground into the large leaves of the plant.

"When your mother...went away...did you talk to her?"

"Of course, I did. I begged Mama not to go."

"And what did she say?"

"She grunted that I was ready. Ready!"

"Uh-huh."

"I tried to reason with her but she told me to stop whining. Then she hushed me, said she sensed trouble and told my brother and me to climb a tree. I told her we were brown bears, not black bears, and that black bears climbed trees, not brownies like us. She told me to quit being smart, slapped us on our behinds and told us to hide in the bushes. Then she ran off."

My breathing was labored, moisture was clouding my eyes, a marmot was stuck in my throat.

"And?" Dr. Chordata urged.

"We hid in the bushes for days waiting for her. It was cold and we were hungry and we could hear the wolves howling all night long."

"Go on."

I sat up shaking, my mouth dry, all 42 of my teeth grinding together. A cub-like sound, the hoarse bark of a fox, coughed out of my mouth.

"She never came back..."

Dr. Chordata leaned forward.

"Then what did you do?"

"With our noses to the ground we searched for days for her. We found her in a meadow flirting with a huge male who looked like he weighed ten thousand pounds. They were wrestling with their forelegs. He was biting my mom on her face and her neck and her shoulders. She was biting back, laughing. Then he...he..."

"Then he what?"

I stood up, tilted my head back and moaned.

"I think that's enough for today, Mr. Brown."

I AM INSIDE THE BEAR PLUG INN, A BROWN BEAR BAR burrowed out of basalt near the border of the borough. A sign behind the bar reads:

PROUDLY POURING PURE BEAR'S MILK
GUARANTEED 30 PERCENT FAT CONTENT

My brother Teddy is bartending, serving frothy buckets of bear milk while he chugs a mug or two for himself. Big Bear is holding court at the end of the bar, telling stories to the crowd.

"So Bobby Bear asked me the most unusual place I've mated and I said, 'That would have to be up the bay, Bob,' when I..."

Big Bear notices me and stops his story. The bar goes silent.

"What did I tell you about coming in here, kid?" he says.

"C'mon, B.B., just a little taste, one for the trail," I beg through slurred words.

"You've had enough mamas' milk, kid, go sleep it off."

"I can't sleep, I need a drink," I say, heating up.

"You're barred from this bar, Brownie," Big Bear says. "Beat it."

Powerful paws grab me from behind and drag me out of the bar. I look up to see my mother as she dumps me in the gravel. She dusts off her paws, then walks back into the bar. I curl up, shaking. I feel the eyes of a thousand wolves watching me from the forest.

"I SENSE YOU CARRY A LOT OF ANGER TOWARD your mother."

"Wow, Doc, you're smarter than the average bear."

"Sarcasm is often a defense against pain."

"I'm not in pain, I'm just angry."

"I wonder if some of this anger is misdirected."

"Misdirected? A defense against pain? If I had a mother who had done her job I wouldn't be sitting here today."

"The infant mortality rate is thirty-five percent in the first year, Mr. Brown."

"Your point?" I said, resting the back of my head on my paws, staring up at the passing clouds.

"Didn't she feed and protect you?"

"By scaring us to death?"

"Scaring you? Tell me more about that."

"Always telling us about the predictions of that crazy 15th century French bear."

"Nostrafursus?"

"Yes. Once upon a time, she would say, a bear could safely walk through the woods, but then, just like Nostrafursus said, the death squads came, with coats like trees and bushes, stalking bears, murdering us as if we were creatures of no significance. All male bears are to blame for the death squads, Mama said. She also told us the crazy Frog bear predicted that young male bears that disobey their mothers would be abducted in the middle of hibernation, made to dance for our food before our gall bladders were cut out and shipped to faraway lands."

Dr. Chordata sat quietly for a moment.

"Is your mother still alive?"

"Oh, yes."

"When did you last see her?"

"Ten years ago."

"So you're 12 ½ now... you haven't seen her since she left?"

"Correct."

"How do you know she's still alive?"

"I can smell her a mile away."

I AM WALKING IN THE FOREST AND THE SMELL OF HONEY draws me to a cabin. The sweet aroma is intoxicating; I sway to and fro on my back legs like I've seen humans do with their bottles around the campfire at night. I shatter the cabin door. Humans scream as they dive through windows and curl up in balls. My paws stick to the floor as I move around, ripping open cupboards, overturning tables. Honey is oozing down the walls, flooding the floors. I'm in heaven. The more honey I eat the more pours from the cabin.

A female scent tickles my nose. Driven by urges I start down a hallway the length of an ice field. In the distance a bevy of sexy female bears lay under a giant cottonwood tree, snacking on a rack of moose. They wink at me, enticing me forward with their foreclaws.

Yes! I run for them but I'm in slow motion, my legs stuck in the honey. The harder I try, the deeper I sink. A long legged blondish bear runs her tongue along her teeth while a female with a reddish coat scratches her claws along the branch, leaving a groove in the bark. I'm sinking deeper, the honey up to my chest, thick against my belly, matting my fur. The females frown at me, begin to pout. I call to them but the honey is pouring into my mouth, gagging me. Don't go I say, but I'm drowning in the honey. They turn away from me and gnaw on the moose bones.

"TODAY I WOULD LIKE TO TALK ABOUT YOUR relationships with the opposite sex."

I fidgeted in the grass. A ground squirrel raced by and I snatched it and bit off its head and offered the body to Dr. Chordata.

"No, thank you. You are almost 13 and you are still a...well, you haven't mated yet."

I shrugged, looked down at the patch of purple lupine between my feet.

"A male bear is ready to breed by the age of five."

"Thanks for reminding me, Doc," I said as I absent-mindedly began digging a hole in front of me.

"I notice you're digging again, Mr. Brown. Remember our agreement on digging? You destroy my office floor every week."

I paused and caught my breath. I had dug five feet beneath the ground. I popped my head up and shoved dirt out of the way.

"I'm depressed."

"Uh-huh. Let's talk about your weekend. How was your date with Cinnamon?"

I snorted, kicked dirt back in the hole.

"You two did go out again, yes?"

"Yeah."

"And what happened on your date?"

"Dinner."

"Good. Tell me more about that."

"I took her to the new restaurant at 10-mile with the salmon spawning stream running through the joint. We both had the rotting-log-stuffed-with-insects special."

"Yum."

"After dinner we swam across the Chilkat to the flats and walked along and talked. Next thing I know she's tripped me with her foreleg and she's biting me on my neck."

"Uh, huh, oh, my," my therapist said, fanning herself with a paw.

"Then we wrestled, bit each other some more..." I said, my voice trailing off.

"Aaaaand?"

"Nothing. I got upset, knocked down a stand of alder trees. It was her fault."

"Her fault? She wasn't ready? The female sometimes waits four or five dates before mating."

"Oh, she was ready, all right."

"Uh-huh."

I stared down in silence, swatting away a swarm of mosquitoes. Suddenly I jumped into the hole and dug furiously.

"Work on anger, Mr. Brown, let's work on anger."

Every time she sways her little tail at me
It brings out the male in me
I'm in love with the bear next door

I AM ON STAGE AT THE CHILKAT VALLEY CENTER OF THE Ursine Arts. I am dressed in black tie and tuxedo, a bowler cocked to one side, my paws spread open, singing to the sold-out crowd.

When we're dancing claw to claw
Ooooooh, there oughta be a law
I'm in love with the bear next door

Cinnamon enters stage left. Her eyes sparkle in the center of her classically beautiful dish-shaped face. Her reddish-brown coat shimmers like a sunset. The audience roars as she breaks into song:

Until he tells me I'm his mate
I will wait and hibernate
I'm in love with the bear next door

Paw to paw, claws entwined, we dance back and forth across the stage, spinning and twirling, the crowd on its back legs clapping its forelegs together. I dip her low to the stage floor, holding one paw while she extends her other to the audience and sings:

My head screams out 'beware!'
But my heart just doesn't care
I'm in love with the bear next door

The next verse is mine but when I try to sing nothing comes out. I'm confused, sweating, afraid. My throat is dry. Cinnamon, always the professional, mouths my next line but I can't hear. I feel the tension in the theater as the crowd huffs and puffs. I watch in slow motion as a salmon carcass flies through the air and lands on the stage in front of me. Then another salmon. The lower leg of a moose hits me on the head, a paw full of blueberries splatter in my face. Now the theater is raining on me. Fish skeletons, Devil's Club bushes, soapberries, old backpacks fly onto the stage. Humiliated, Cinnamon runs off the stage.

DR. CHORDATA COULD BE AS IRRITATING AS A MILE long tapeworm, but maybe she was right on one point: my anger was a large beaver dam blocking the flow of my life. Huff ten times before I react, she told me. Be aware of situations that trigger my anger. Take control of my life.

The mating season was closing and soon my urges would turn exclusively to food and to bulking up for the winter. Now was my last chance to consummate my relationship with Cinnamon. In the morning I brushed the thorns and nettles from my coat and rubbed salmon oil on my face and neck. Visualize, think positive, make affirmations, Dr. Chordata had told me. Standing on the riverbank I stared at my reflection in the water. Who's the bear? I'm the bear!

I swam across the river, heading toward Cinnamon's range on the other side of the valley. I walked through the alder and willow brush, the color of the leaves softening as fall approached. I swam a few more channels until I reached the flats. I came out of the freezing water invigorated. I was confident and strong and ready. Who's the bear? I'm the bear!

Cinnamon was facing away from me, eating a salmon. Her sensual behind beckoned to me as I snuck up on her. I gnawed at her back leg. She puffed a few breaths as she turned toward me. She jumped back.

"Oh, hi, Brownie," she said, looking around.

"Hi, Cinnamon, you act surprised," I laughed, my stomach tightening. I noticed her fur was rumpled. I tried to nip at her neck but she pushed me away.

"We need to talk," Cinnamon said.

"I'm ready now, honey. Let's talk later."

"I think it's time we see other bears," Cinnamon said. A familiar feeling of emptiness ran through me. A shiver of ice descended through my body.

"I don't want to see other bears," I said.

She looked at me, her silence stronger than words. I moved toward her again but she held up her paws.

"Please, Brownie, don't make this any more difficult. This relationship isn't working out for both of us and..."

"Things have changed, Cinnamon. I'm a new bear."

"...and you're scaring me," she said.

I heard steps in the gravel. I looked up to my left and a big bear walked toward Cinnamon with a salmon in his mouth. He didn't notice me as he dropped the fish in front of her.

"Hey, honey, here's another salmon for my little salmonberry," he said.

"My little salmonberry?" I said, bees starting to buzz in my head.

"Who's this?" I said, my heart rate rising.

"A...a friend," Cinnamon said.

I took a step toward the bear.

"You got a name...friend?" I said, loosening my neck and shoulders.

"I got a name," he replied, standing on his back legs and sniffing the air around me. "Smells like you've got a problem."

"I'm a problem solver," I said as I hooked him in the head with my left paw. As he stumbled I dug my teeth into his shoulder, ripped out a piece of fur and pushed him into the river. He stood up, put his paw to his shoulder and looked at the blood.

"You bit me," he said in disbelief.

He charged me and we rolled and tumbled, biting, scratching and pounding on each other. Ribs cracked and bones broke. Cinnamon yelled for us to stop but we were beyond words. I got on top of him and pinned him, pummeling him with a thunderstorm of paw strikes. He slid out from under me and rumbled into the trees.

"Okay, Cinnamon," I said, turning toward her, but she was gone. I saw the blur of her behind as she raced across the mudflats.

"MR. BROWN, ARE YOU OKAY?"

"I've lost my sense of smell."

"That can be a challenge for us bears."

"Yes, a challenge to go along with my forty puncture wounds, a wide hole in my chest, broken ribs, a broken nose, a dislocated shoulder and a cracked skull."

"Tell me about it."

"I slipped on a salmon carcass."

"Uh-huh."

We sat in silence. I waited for her to ask me a question. Finally I spoke. "Mating is overrated."

"What aspect of mating do you find overrated?" Dr. Chordata asked.

"All of it."

"I wonder how you arrived at that conclusion."

I shot the doctor a dirty look and raked the ground with my claws.

"Mr. Brown, do you want to talk about what happened to you? This is a small valley. I know about your fight with another bear over Cinnamon. Stop at any salmon stream or berry patch and one can hear all the gory details."

I stood up and clacked my teeth.

"If I hadn't listened to you I wouldn't have this problem!"

I quickly dug a three-foot-deep hole and sat in it. Dr. Chordata paused and exhaled a deep flow of breath.

"Believe me, Mr. Brown, blaming bears for your bad behavior is not the answer to your problem. The blame for your bad behavior rests on your shoulder blades. We bears are not angry by nature. That's an anti-Ursinic myth that humans have used against bears for years as an excuse to murder us and you're basically buying into that b.s."

I stood up from my hole and paced.

"Let's talk about choices."

"Okay," I said, ripping an elderberry bush from the ground. "Here's a choice for you. I'm choosing to leave the Chilkat Valley."

"Where are you going?"

"I don't know. Somewhere in the Lower 48, like Colorado or California, where a bear can get a fair shake."

"And you think going there will make a difference?"

"Nothing I do here makes a difference."

"Moving to another range won't resolve a bear's issues."

I stopped pacing and turned to Dr. Chordata.

"Wasting my time with you week after week hasn't resolved any issues, either."

As I stormed from Dr. Chordata's office I fell into the hole I had dug. I jumped out and stomped through the brush. I heard her voice behind me.

"Good luck, Mr. Brown. Be careful of falling into the holes you dig."

I LIMPED ALONG ABOVE THE TREE LINE, LOOKING down on the valley. Good riddance, I thought. I couldn't wait to get away from the negativity of my old range. California, here I come! I'd heard the humans in California loved brown bears so much they put an image of us on their state flag. I saw myself sitting by a pristine river with a sweet sow feeding me berries as I dipped my feet in a cool stream on a hot summer day.

Pain sliced into my injured shoulders as I moved downhill toward the river. My left fore leg gave out on me and I tumbled end over end. I hit a tree, bounced off a stump, smashed into another tree, rolled through a thicket of Devil's Club, the plants thorns ripping at my fur. I knew a cliff edge was near but I couldn't slow my momentum.

There was a brief euphoric flash when I fell off the edge, a feeling of weightlessness and peace and freedom, before I dropped like a boulder. I let out a painful moan as I landed on a car parked on the side of the road. I lay there, the violence of the impact echoing through my body. I tentatively flexed my muscles, checking for new injuries.

I heard high pitched whimpers, like a coyote's, and I hoped the sounds weren't coming from me. The voices came from inside the car. I lowered my head to look inside. Two humans, a male and a female, were curled up together in the back of the car. When they saw me they screamed. I'd never seen humans without their coats on.

It wasn't pretty.

I slid off the car and dragged my body across the road to the river. The chill in the air told me the glaciers had slowed their melting, lowering the level of the rivers, but without my sense of smell I had no sense of direction. Walking along the mudflats, disoriented, I understood for the first time what it was like to be lost. When I reached an island full of cottonwoods, the crushing weight of ten years of little sleep and bad dreams and lost hope landed on me like an old-growth spruce tree. I passed out.

I WATCH MYSELF AS I AM WHEELED, APPARENTLY unconscious, into the emergency room of the Cedar-Spruce-Hemlock Medical Center. A black bear wearing a jacket with "BEARMEDIC" on the back pushes me toward Triage.

"This bear needs immediate attention!" the bearmedic yells.

A bored brown bear nurse, chewing on a bone, tosses paperwork on the desk.

"Fill out his managed bear care information and have a seat."

The bearmedic leans in close on the nurse.

"This bear is going into hibernation!"

The nurse drops her bone and rushes from behind the desk.

"Why didn't you say so?"

The bearmedic and the nurse wheel me through swinging doors and down a hallway full of bear doctors and nurses.

"Code Brown, bears! Code Brown!" the nurse screams.

I am surrounded by a surgical team as shiny instruments are passed back and forth. The head surgeon holds his paws up in front of him while an assistant files his claws to a sharp, gleaming edge.

"Nurse, how's the patient?"

"Pulse is at eight, down from forty beats per minute; temperature is ninety, down from 110; respiratory rate is two, down from ten breaths per minute."

The head surgeon nods grimly. He looks around.

"He's hibernating, all right. Where's the DeHibernation Unit?"

A Brown Bear Brass Band struts into the operating room and circles the bed. I have a tuba in one ear, a trombone in the other and trumpets in my face. The head surgeon lays his razor sharp claws on my stomach.

"On three...one...two...three!"

The band blasts its music at me and the surgeon tickles me with his claws. I leap up, eyes wide open, holding my paws to my ears.

"I'm tired of this! I want to go to sleep!" I yell at the doctor.

The doctor, still tickling me, removes his surgical mask. It is Dr. Chordata. She shakes her head at me.

"Good boy bears can't go to sleep until they clean up their dens and yours is a mess from all the holes you've dug."

"I want to go to sleep!" I yell again as the drummer from the band clashes his cymbals in my ears.

"TAKE NAPS NOW YOU WON'T BE ABLE TO SLEEP ALL winter." I woke up, a voice from long ago beating on my eardrums. I was face down in the mud, my nose, ears and mouth full of glacial silt from the river. I shook my head and an avalanche of pain rumbled through my throbbing skull. I sniffed the air, hoping for a connection to the world. Still nothing.

"You lay around in the river bed you'll catch your death of pneumonia."

My body freezes, my stomach tightens.

"But you won't have to worry about that if you don't start eating," the cracking voice continued. "A bear loses fifteen to forty percent of its body weight over the winter. You know that. And watch what you eat. Stay away from that fast food road kill. Full of parasites."

Was I still dreaming? I tested my level of consciousness by pounding my head against the ground. Numbing pain flashed through my body.

"Once upon a time a young bear didn't eat enough for the winter. Wouldn't listen to his mother no matter how many times she told him to eat and eat and eat. He was so thin when he crawled out of his den in the spring an eagle swooped down and carried him off. The eagle tore the meat right off the little bear's bones. Then the eagle lined his nest with the little bear's coat. True story. Should have listened to his mother."

I stumbled to my feet, my legs unsteady. I turned toward the voice. An old sow stood facing me on all fours in the low bushes. Her coat had the dull, grayish blue of the ground cover going to seed on the mountains. Patches of fur were missing, exposing sores on her body.

"I was walking a mile or so upwind of here when I caught a whiff of you and I thought I better check up on how you were doing."

"I'm fine," I said, groaning as I inhaled, my lungs expanding into my cracked ribs. I scratched at the river bed.

"Sure doesn't look like it to me. What are you doing? You're making a mess."

I looked down at the hole I was digging.

"I'm digging."

"Yes, I can tell that. You were always a digger, just like your father."

"What about my father?"

"Oh, please," my mother said, dismissing my question with a wave of her paw. "What a loser. Last I heard he was in the Alaskan Fish and Game Relocation Program. Classic garbageholic. We live in a valley with five types of salmon, three different trout, seventeen kinds of berries and some of the biggest moose in the world. So what does your father do? Spends his days and nights with those other deadbeat dads down at the garbage dump eating human trash. Human food will give you tumors the size of a porcupine's butt."

"You told us baby-eating monsters lived in the garbage dumps," I said, memories flickering in my head.

"And when was the last time you were at the dump?"

"Never."

"It worked, didn't it?"

My mother contorted her round face and limped at me with her paws extended. "I smell the scent of a brown bear cub," she snarled, swiping at me with her claws.

"That's not funny," I said as I felt a smile bubbling up from deep inside me.

My mother sat down beside me and brushed gravel and silt off my face.

"I didn't want you to grow up and be a garbage bear like your father. I knew how hardheaded male bears can be so I felt I had to scare you to prepare you for the world."

"Well," I said, the tension in my body softening.

"Now, you're not hardheaded are you?" my mother said.

I looked down in the water, feeling young and embarrassed.

"Look," my mother said, pointing toward the sinking sun.

We sat together quietly and watched the salmon colored sky slowly darken. As the last rays of light flickered away I fell asleep on my mother's shoulder.

*I AM AT THE FALL SALE AT BED, BEAR, AND BEHIND, A
popular store in the valley. A young human female with blond hair, about the
size of a coyote, greets me. I am surprised when she speaks to me in fluent Bear and
offers me complimentary porridge.*

*"No, thank you," I say, "Porridge is never just right for me. It's always too hot or
too cold."*

We walk over to the bed section.

"These beds have all been slept in," she tells me.

"Obviously," I say.

*"Oh, my," she says, pointing to a small bed, "Look at this Baby Bear bed. Not
too soft, not too hard. It's what I use."*

*"I'm not a baby bear," I say, reeling from her human odor and moving down
wind of her."*

"Oh, my, this is the Mama Bear bed. Very soft."

"No, thanks. I'm not a Mama Bear."

"Oh, my, this is the Papa Bear bed. It can be very hard and difficult to sleep in."

"Let's see."

I crawl into the bed and curl up.

*"This bed is exactly what I've been looking for," I say to the little blonde-haired
human. "This isn't as hard as it looks. I'll take it."*

I WOKE UP AND MY MOTHER WAS GONE. IT WAS morning and soft raindrops pressed on me like squirrel's feet. I stood up and my nose filled with the life of the valley. Yes, my smell was back. I sucked on the sweet scent of the high bush cranberry. The musty smell of decomposing leaves made me dizzy.

I spent the next few weeks eating salmon and berries, putting on ten pounds a day. My beat up body needed plenty of healing so I decided to turn in early for the winter. Next year would be a good year for me, I said to myself as I walked across the valley. I found a well worn trail and headed up the mountain to dig my den. Walking through a densely covered section of the forest I smelled humans up ahead. I slipped behind a stand of alders to avoid scaring them. When the humans were safely down wind I stood up and huffed and puffed. I wanted all the creatures out there to know the news.

Who's the bear? I'm the bear!

MOOSE
A Detective Story

SHE WALKED INTO MY OFFICE, ALL 800 POUNDS OF sweet lean Alaskan moose sashaying my way. A light rust tint sparkled off her golden brown hair. She bent over, stripped a willow branch with her mouth and ate slow, like I wasn't there. She looked up at me. Water lilies danced in the swampy ponds of her eyes.

"I'm Cervida and I'm missing my male."

"I'll bet he's missing you, too."

"That's not what I mean. He's missing. Gone."

"How long has he been gone?"

"Three days."

"That's not long."

"It is for one of my bulls. I tell my males when it's time to be missing and when it's time to be gone."

She turned sideways to grab an alder leaf so I grabbed a look at her body. Her humped shoulder, pale long legs and big head with her overhanging snout sent shivers through the dewlap under my chin. She stepped next to me and looked me up and down.

"You're tall."

I'm a hoof over seven feet at the shoulders and I'm a good 10 feet long.

"Bigger than average," I said.

She nudged my antlers.

"Nice rack. How big is it?"

I flared out my chest and extended my neck so she could get a good look at my six foot wide antlers.

"Way bigger than average," I said.

"I've heard that before," Cervida said, turning to eat more leaves.

"Look, you beautiful cow, you're not here to give me a physical and this ain't no restaurant. So, what can I do for you?"

"I hear you're the best."

"Best at what?"

"Finding things."

"I'm not bad."

"No, you're not."

She chewed the leaf slowly as we stood staring at each other.

"Are you free to find my male?"

"I ain't free and I ain't cheap."

"Neither am I," she said.

I stripped a branch from above me and chewed and stared while she chewed and stared back.

"Sure, Ms. Cervida—"

"Call me Vida."

"Okay, Vida, I'll graze around and see what I can find."

I'M AL GIGAS, MOOSE DETECTIVE. I'VE ROAMED THE mean riverbeds of the Chilkat Valley for ten years and I've seen things no creature should ever see and I've seen creatures that will never see again.

A missing moose is a bad sign but I didn't mention that to Vida. She wasn't the first ungulate to walk into my office looking for a loved one. I've had brothers looking for brothers, calves for mothers, mothers for calves. I find things, Vida was right about that. But what I find this time of year would be better if it stayed lost.

October was almost here. The wind starts blowing out of the north, the kind of wind that raises the inch-long hair on your rump and sends a sick feeling down into your large rumen, the biggest of my four stomachs. When the fall wind blows any meadow can explode with a moose battle; a misunderstood bellow can end with a fight to the death. The north wind tells a moose that winter is coming and life is about to get tougher. And if you're a moose in the Chilkat Valley you know that the wind is telling you the killings are about to begin.

"MUWAH! MUWAH!"

I was thinking less about Vida's male and more about the way she swayed out of my office when I heard the moose call from up valley. Thinking this might have something to do with my case, I trotted up the flats of the Chilkat River, my stomachs growling for food. Vida paid me my usual retainer of 300 pounds of wet forage and I could sure use it. I go through 40 to 50 pounds a day during the summer but as fall nears I can put away 100 pounds a day.

A herd of moose ahead of me milled around in the shallows of the river near a stand of alders. Two bulls together usually means trouble. More than two bulls together means big trouble. Sheriff Winkle stood in front of the others, staring down at the brown, silty river water.

"How are you doing, Sheriff?"

"How am I doing, Gigas? How am I doing? I got more internal parasites than a porcupine's got quills. I got flukes, nematodes and bot flies. I'm a walking worm factory. I got tapeworms, whipworms, bladder worms, nodular worms and lungworms. My lower front teeth are as dull as my brain but not sharp like my upper front teeth."

"Moose don't have upper front teeth, Sheriff."

"You're sharp, Gigas. You should be a detective."

The sheriff pointed his antlers toward the moose crowd.

"Go tell us what you think about the mess over there, detective."

I knew what I thought and I knew what I was going to find and I knew it wasn't going to be pretty. No matter how many times you see it you never get used to seeing a member of your species massacred. I walked to the moose, the herd stepping back to let me through.

"Lots of blood," I said.

"Blood! I knew it!" someone said.

I looked up. There's always one dumb moose in the crowd.

"That could have been me," a moose said, his voice shaking.

"Could have been any one of us," I said, "and next time it will be one of us."
The moose mooed a collective moo.

"What kind of animal would do something like this?"

I shrugged my shoulders as I circled the drying pool of blood. I could tell the victim was a bull because of the tracks. A male moose has a longer hoof because he tends to be a third larger than a female. A male hoof is also blunter at the front end whereas a female hoof has a sharp point. A cow track has a circular outline but a bull track is more oblong. I knew he had tried to run away from his killer because of the wide stride marks in the mud. Our walking stride is 3.5 to 5.5 feet but when we trot or run our stride lengthens to 8 feet.

"Hmm," I said.

"What's that mean?" a voice behind me asked.

"It means 'hmm.' It also means our victim was surprised and he tried to run away before he was attacked."

"How do you know?"

"Lucky guess."

I followed the death stain, the mixture of blood and mud forming a cloudy sunset on the ground. The trail ended in a set of familiar tracks. Tire tracks, from a human truck. A flash of lightning stung my brain and I stumbled, memory kicking up swirls of dust in my head.

"You okay, Al?"

I steadied myself and nodded my antlers.

"Yeah, just lost my footing is all. Just lost my footing."

COWS ARE MY WEAKNESS, AND OF ALL THE VALLEYS in all of Alaska and the Yukon, she had to walk into mine. Male moose are able to mate at two-years-old but I was almost four and I hadn't mated yet even though I told my friends that I had. Not that I hadn't tried, but the older bulls were too tough. They intimidated me, pushed me around, kicked mud in my face.

I was walking through the brush during mating season, late September, resigning myself to a loveless life when I stopped in my tracks. I lifted my chin, stretched my neck, opened my mouth wide. The nasal organ in my upper palate pumped mucus and I captured a whiff of airborne chemicals telling me a female was nearby. The old Flehman's Response.

She stepped out of the trees into the clearing in the meadow. She was thin and frail. Her two inch tail wagged back and forth, her long ears turned in the wind. I got a case of the gulps and she turned toward me.

"Oh, great, another one," she said.

She turned up her overhanging nose and lip.

"How unusual. A salivating, chomping, lip-smacking male moose that makes a hollow gulping sound every two seconds. How charming. I feel faint."

Embarrassed, I wiped my mouth on the brush.

"Let me guess. You're going to create a shallow depression in the ground, paw the earth into a muddy mess and expect me to lie down and roll around in it?"

"Hey, I'm only out for a walk and you walked into my path."

"Then keep walking and don't get any ideas."

I walked a few steps away from her and stopped, full of ideas.

"Uh, do you like pond scum?"

"Is this a trick question? Who doesn't?"

Nervous, I looked down and kicked a few rocks.

"I know a spot that has the best pond scum in the valley and I thought you might...want to come along."

She gave me the moose stare. I looked up at the sky, down valley, up valley. I stole a sideways glance at her. She was still staring.

"Well?"

"Don't rush me, I'm thinking. Well, okay, that sounds good. I've been eating willow all day and I'm sick of it. But, hey, keep your hooves to yourself."

We walked in silence through the woods, stopping now and then to nibble on the fading flora. When we came to the watering hole she jumped in.

"Oh, yum, delicious," she said, her snout stained green. "It's so salty. I love it."

The way she slurped at the algae made me wish I was pond scum.

"The food in the ponds and lakes has 400 times the salt of the twigs we eat during the winter," I told her. "That's why we need to stock up on sodium rich foods during the summer and fall."

"You're a smart one," she said.

"I know things."

"Hmm."

"What's that mean?"

"It means, 'hmm,'" she said.

We spent the next few days grazing from pond to pond and slough to slough. She was nervous and sensitive, jumping at the slightest noises in the night. She told me about her traumatic youth. Most moose are born in late May or early June, but she arrived in July and only weighed 15 pounds, less than half my birth weight. She wasn't even 100 pounds by the fall and she barely survived her first winter. She couldn't remember long segments of her early life until she went to regressive memory therapy and relived seeing a brown bear eat her mother.

She was two and a half years old but she was not much bigger than a yearling and I had an overwhelming drive to protect her. She was stunning and I kept my gulping to a minimum while I was with her but it wasn't easy. I bit my lip to stop chomping and smacking but that's hard to do when you don't have upper front teeth.

I was on my best behavior, waiting for her to give me a sign. One evening we stood near a road, munching on greens, the sky scorched red by the setting sun. She rubbed her rump against mine and whispered in my ear, "Moo-moo-ah, moo-moo-ah."

Are there sweeter words in any language? I romanced her for a week. We rolled in the mud and swam in the rivers. I was singing a song I'd written for her, "My Baby's Got Me in a Rut," when the wind started blowing slowly from the north. She nuzzled up close to me.

"The north wind," she shivered, "it gives me a bad feeling."

"It's just the wind."

We were standing in silence watching the last rays of the sun dip behind the mountains when I heard the clumsy sound of human footsteps. She was still naïve about the dangers of the world and looked upon humans as harmless, funny looking creatures.

I knew better.

"Look," she said, laughing, "they're so...goofy."

Then I saw the flash of metal from the guns.

"Run!" I said. "Follow me!"

I ran through the thicket, breaking small trees in my path. A gunshot blasted through the air, the sound stinging my ears. As the ringing echoed away all I could hear was the lonely sound of my hooves on the soft earth of the rainforest. My stomachs spasmed as I turned my head to look for her. She was laying on the ground, eyes open, blood drooling out her mouth. The approach of human footsteps stole my time to grieve and I ran into the woods until I was exhausted.

I spent the night in the forest, walking in circles, smashing my antlers against tree trunks, hoping that the impact would awaken me from a bad dream. But this was no dream and in the morning my nightmare continued. I walked back to the spot where she had been shot, but her body was gone. I followed her blood trail, sucking in the last wisps of her scent as her sweet smell disappeared into the greenery around me. Then I looked down.

At the tire tracks in the road.

"YOU OKAY, GIGAS?"

The sheriff's voice brought me back from my thoughts.

"Sure, I'm fine."

"Everyone go on about your business," the sheriff told the herd. "It's mating season. Go have some fun, but be careful out there."

The moose bellowed, smacked antlers and headed their own ways. I turned to the sheriff.

"Go have some fun?"

"That's right, Gigas. Let them go have some fun. While they can. You stopped having fun a long time ago."

"What about the murder?"

"What about it? What do you expect me to do? Catch the murderer? Bring him to justice? What world do you live in?"

I shrugged my shoulders.

"Listen, Gigas, you're hired to find missing moose, right, Gigas? Lucky you. I'm hired to keep moose from being missed. Unlucky me. We're just moose and the odds are against us. The sun starts to set on us the day we're born and we have to catch as much daylight as we can before nightfall. I'm here to give some kind of order to the exit line."

"You saying we have no control over our destiny, Sheriff?"

"None, my friend, not a bit. Don't take it personal. It is what it is."

I nodded my head and slowly headed down the river bank.

"Where you going, Al?"

"To take control of my destiny, Sheriff."

"SEE ANYTHING TODAY?"

"Nope, not me. I haven't seen a thing in months."

"I find that hard to believe."

"Believe what you will."

I was talking to Hal, a bald eagle perched on a cottonwood tree with a clear view of the murder scene.

"How's your hearing?" I asked.

"What's that?" Hal said. We looked at each other and chuckled.

"Listen, wise one, a brother moose was killed down by the flats within the last 12 hours. What do you know?"

"I know better than to get involved with the humans during the killing season."

"So the murderer was a human?"

"I didn't say that."

"What are you afraid of? You're an American bald eagle. You're protected."

"Oh, yeah? My cousin mouthed off one too many times and next thing you know his wings are clipped and he's doing life in one of those prisons where the humans stare at you all day."

"Better than having them shoot and stuff you like the old days."

"Just a slower death, Mr. Detective."

The sound of a distant gun shot echoed off the mountains. Hal shook his feathers.

"Too close for me. I'm out of here."

With a flap of his wings Hal dropped off his branch and soared up valley. I snuck through the trees toward the sound of the gun. When I heard the fading murmur of human voices in the woods I stopped and waited for silence. Then I walked into a clearing and stepped into a pool of blood. I shook my legs and tried to wipe them on the ground but the blood had already stained my hooves. An engine started up on the other side of the willows and I ran toward the sound. A white truck was driving away on the dirt road. I wanted to tail the truck and discover where it was going but the dust from the road choked and disoriented me. I lost my footing and slid coughing into a ravine. I looked up into the fog of dirt, blinded by my eternal nightmare.

COULD I HAVE DONE ANYTHING TO PROTECT HER? That's always the question that rips at my heart like a bear claw. Should I have told her to run ahead of me? Should I have charged the humans and caught them off guard? I'm a tough moose, at least that's my reputation. I sent a brown bear to the Promise Land with a powerful kick to the head. I gored a male alpha wolf with my antlers and tossed him in the river. He wasn't an alpha wolf after that.

What ifs and could have beens banged antlers in my head. The sheriff was right. We're moose. We live 15 years on this earth, we're lucky. We die of old age we're blessed. If the bears don't eat us when we're young they'll eat us when we're old. If the humans don't shoot us when we're at the peak of our lives the wolves will take us down when we're tired and feeble. We're herbivores in a carnivore world. It is what it is.

I walked along the river toward town as twilight dimmed the valley. As I neared town I stood alongside the road tucked back into the trees, scanning the trucks as they came and went. Which truck held the human that killed my love? Which truck was responsible for today's murder? Were all the humans in all the trucks responsible for all the moose murders over the years?

As night settled in around me I crept into town, avoiding the well-lit areas. A light rain patted my coat. I walked the trails between the human homes, looking at trucks and examining the tracks left by their tire treads. Was it this one? No, that one? Maybe that one? The problem was the trucks all looked alike, just like humans all look alike. And if I did find the killer what was I going to do? I'm a moose detective. Just thinking of the species jurisdictional issues gave me a headache.

I stood in a field of dying fireweed and cow's parsnip. The stars shimmered above me and the moon lit up the water in front of me. I looked over the fields of food and tried to understand carnivore mentality. What more could they want than this? I shook my head.

I PACED BACK AND FORTH IN MY OFFICE IN MOOSE
Meadows for the next few days. I didn't go out. No one came in. I couldn't
get the bloodstains off my hooves. My head ached, each gunshot in the
distance a dull roar in my head, reminding me of the killings.

The past sat on my chest like a 1200 pound brown bear. I couldn't
predict the future and I obviously couldn't forget the past, but I knew I
could find Cervida's male if he was still alive. She had given me his general
range, a ten mile area between my office and the town. However, to get
that close to town during the killing season was suicide this time of year. I
might as well hang a "shoot me" sign from my antlers. But I had a job to do.

I knew I would have to stop for lunch nine or ten times, so I walked
out of the meadows mid-afternoon and grazed my way toward town. At
one point I was spooked by what I thought was a human truck but it was
only a car with gray maned humans staring at me. I stared back until they
drove off.

Focus, Gigas, I mumbled to myself. I had to be more careful so I moved
further into the woods. I looked for moose landmarks: fresh moose
scat, newly broken alder branches, muddy, hooved tracks. I stopped for
another bite to eat. I knew better than to waste my time chasing a moose. If
he was alive he would come my way. I was in his range. I finished chewing
and closed my eyes and slowly dozed off.

"I'VE GOT THE HERBIVORE BLUES."

> *"Moo-moo-ah, moo-moo-ah."*
> *"Tell those carnivores the news."*
> *"Moo-moo-ah, moo-moo-ah."*

I was standing at the bar at Rumen's Café. The banner above the stage read: Vida and The Dream Cows. Cervida sashayed her rump back and forth across the stage as her cows mooed behind her.

> *"They say it is what it is*
> *That it just beez that way*
> *And if there's no tomorrow*
> *I need some lovin' today*
> *I've got the herbivore blues*
> *Hey, girls, can I get some help?"*

The Dream Cows swung their short tails back and forth, singing:

> *"Moo-moo-ah, moo-moo-ah."*

A spotlight followed Vida as she slowly walked off the stage and came my way. The Dream Cows kept the rhythm:

> *"Moo-moo-ah, moo-moo-ah."*
> *"Tell the carnivores the news*
> *I've got the herbivore blues*

Why don't they get a clue
They're giving me, oh,
The carnivores are giving me
The herbivore blues!"

Vida had snuggled in next to me, eye to eye, snout to snout, as she held that last b-flat note. With her this close her female hormones should have filled my nasal cavity with mucus, but there was no Flehman's Response.

Somewhere a twig snapped and woke me from my dream. I spun around. A young, small bull was standing there, squinting at me.

"YOU AL GIGAS?"

"Depends."

"On what?"

"On who you are."

"I'm a friend of Vida and I hear you're looking for me."

"Then I'm Al Gigas."

He bent down and chewed on a few dogwood leaves. There was something soft about him, almost feminine. He was passive, unlike most bulls during the rut, or mating season. If you're a male moose, you not only have to be afraid of the humans, but also of the bulls who battle to win the females.

I looked at him. He circled around me four or five times. His hips were stiff and he bumped into a tree as if he didn't see it. He paused and locked eyes with me and stared.

"Where have you been?" I asked.

"Wandering."

"Wandering where?"

"Nowhere in particular."

He started to circle me again.

"Cervida's worried about you. Thinks you might be hurt."

"I'm okay," he said.

"Right," I said. "As okay as a moose with parelaphostrongylus tenuis can be."

His neck twitched.

"I don't know what you're talking about," he said as he circled me again.

"Don't play dumb moose with me," I said. "You've got brainworm, a meningeal flatworm common but not fatal in white-tailed deer. In moose, elk and caribou, we're not so lucky. The parasites live in the eyes and in the central nervous system. The symptoms are repetitive circling, aimless wandering, partial paralysis of the hindquarters and partial blindness."

"You're talking out the side of your snout," he said, talking to a low lying limb of a big spruce tree.

"I'm over here," I said.

He turned toward the sound of my voice, slumped his shoulders in defeat and lowered his antlers.

"All right. Tell Cervida you found me and I was dead."

"Why would I tell her that?"

"Because I told you to tell her that. I don't want her to see me this way."

"Listen, pal. It's rare when I find a live moose during the killing season and it's even rarer when a moose has a chance to say goodbye before he dies. Cervida's a good cow and this ain't no way to treat a cow."

He nodded his head a few times as he circled and limped and bumped into trees.

"You got a way with words, Gigas."

Then I remembered the other symptom of brainworm and the thought sent a shiver of instinct through my body.

"Wait a minute. Another symptom of brainworm is no fear of humans."

"Yeah," he said, "humans ain't so bad. They don't scare me."

"You run across any lately?"

"Down on the road, just a few minutes ago. A couple of males in a white truck. Seemed like nice fellows."

The gunshot roared from somewhere in the trees. Cervida's male blew out a breath as he stumbled once, and then collapsed. I froze for a moment, stunned by the speed of life to death. I looked into his far away eyes, the blood flowing out his mouth, the familiar scene tearing at me. The second shot pierced my rack, blowing off the tip of one of my tines. My blood spurted in the air and sprayed the trees. I bolted away from the sound of the gun, moving blindly through the forest, ripping down small alders and stomping on the thorny Devil's Club bushes. The forest grew darker as I ran deeper and deeper, my head down, driven by the sick feeling of fear.

I smashed into a big, old spruce tree. My long, skinny legs wobbled back and forth. My head spun into darkness.

THE NORTH WIND SLAMMED ME, KNOCKING ME
backwards and off my legs into the river bank. I was blinded by the river
silt, blowing into my eyes like hard, horizontal rain. I stood up on my front
legs and the wind slapped me back to the ground. I lay there, helpless,
pinned to the earth.

The wind stopped. The dust settled as I struggled to stand up. I blinked the
dirt out of my eyes and shook my head a few times to clear my vision. The quiet
in the valley made my stomachs queasy. I looked up. I was in the middle of the
valley and I should have been along the wide, braided Chilkat River but the
riverbed was dry. There was no vegetation; not a baby alder tree or a horsetail
fern. I looked up higher on the Chilkat Mountains and the forest of spruce and
hemlock that once filled the valley was gone. No waterfalls. No snowpack. The
Coast Range, once full of glaciers, stood out like dried animal bones.

I hurt from hunger as I wandered down the dusty riverbed. I stumbled over
what I thought was a big piece of driftwood. When I was about to kick it out of
my way I realized it was a set of decomposing moose antlers. Next to the antlers
was the faint outline of tire tracks. As I followed along slowly, examining the
tread, I recognized the familiar tire patterns in the dirt. My adrenaline kicked
in and I raced along the tracks, running as fast as I could. I ran for miles,
my head down, the tracks becoming crystal clear in front of me. I knew I
was closing in.

My antlers crashed into the back of the white truck, shattering the glass of
the taillights. I dropped to the ground. I smelled the stench of humans and felt
them lift me off the ground and into the back of the truck.

"Hi, Al."

I opened my eyes. Sheriff Winkle was standing over me.

"It is what it is, Al, it is what it is."

I woke up, aching in the dark. I heard the stroke of eagle wings over the treetops. The sound of the leaves blowing in the wind tickled my ears.

A flying squirrel was sitting on my antlers.

"WHAT HAPPENED, AL?"

"Looks like a squirrel mugged me."

Rodney was a Southeast Alaskan flying squirrel, a nocturnal resident of the rain forest. He was a special agent of the Squirrel Burrow of Investigation (SBI) and quite a celebrity in the forest world since he cracked the famous Spruce Cone Caper.

Spruce cones are a major part of a squirrel's diet. One squirrel can store and eat over 16,000 cones a year. When spruce cones began to disappear and there were a series of daring robberies of squirrel caches, the forest roared with the chittering of hungry squirrels. Tempers flared, accusations were made, vigilante justice erupted. Rodney negotiated tense hostage situations as he tried to calm the community. He knew it was an outside job.

Rodney was a master of disguise and he spoke 30 regional squirrel dialects. Posing as a Latvian chipmunk he infiltrated the Russian Rodent Mob. In an action packed, heart stopping, tree top chase through an old growth forest, Stoney battled Boris, the Russian mob leader. Two quick blows from Rodney's lethal tail knocked the rodent gangster from a branch and he plunged two hundred feet to the forest floor, impaling himself on the quills of a local porcupine.

"How did you find me, Rod?"

"Human punk kids have been taking potshots at squirrels so I put together an Automotive Pit Crew Task Force (APCTF) to get under car hoods and chew on wire. We were in the middle of a team meeting a few trees down when I heard the crash."

I wobbled to my feet.

"What do you need from me, Al?"

"I need you to meet me in town later."

"I'm nocturnal, Al. I don't do mornings."

"A moose I was hired to find was killed in the woods a few hours ago. I need to know if anybody saw a truck carrying a stiff moose."

"I've got a couple of crows who are snitches. If they don't know, they know somebody who does."

Rodney took off flying from tree to tree. I ran ten miles to town. I didn't stop once, even to eat. I came up the hill from the river and looked out over the town. I had walked through the little town many times in the middle of the night. Those had been peaceful times for me; serene moments of what life must have been like before humans walked this land. But it wasn't peaceful to me now. Too much blood had been spilled. I was angry.

And full of revenge.

I STOOD UNDER A STREETLIGHT IN FRONT OF THE bank and looked at my reflection in the windows. The top of my right rack was gone, blown away by the shots in the woods. The crash into the tree had tweaked my rack so the left side of my antlers stuck up higher than the right side. Rain ran down the windows of the bank, giving my reflection a distorted, dreamy appearance, as if my physical wounds symbolized my emotional battle scars.

"Pssst. Caw-caw. Psst. Caw-caw."

I turned around. I could make out the outline of a crow in the shadows. I moved toward him.

"Hold your horses, hoofer," the crow said. "Rodney tells me you're looking for info on a moose kill from last night."

"Who are you?" I asked.

"I'm a black bird of the corvid family, often confused with the raven, known for its raucous sound that doesn't have time for small talk. Go down the street past the grocery store and the school. The first street after the Moose Lodge take a right. Three houses down you'll see a white truck. That's who you're looking for."

"Thanks."

"Don't thank me. As far as anyone is concerned, I wasn't here."

"Who wasn't here?"

"Exactly," the crow said as he flew away.

I walked up Main Street, first light softening the mountains around me. A police car patrolled up and down the street on its nightly route. I stepped back into the shadows by the school and hid behind the totem pole out front. After the car passed I looked both ways, then I ran across the street.

The white truck sat in the driveway. I walked up and looked in the back. The smell of blood and death gagged me and I backed up.

The door of the house opened. A human male stepped outside. With a gun. My survival instinct kicked in and, head down, I charged toward him. My speed surprised him. He tried to back up but he stumbled and fell, the rifle falling out of his reach. He got to his knees and I knocked him over on his back. He stumbled to his feet and ran toward a tree. I could have overtaken him but he was no longer a threat. He jumped for a tree limb, missed and slid down the bark. He tried again with no success. My adrenalin slowed and I was able to think beyond instinct. I stepped toward him and stopped ten feet away. He turned to face me. His eyes opened wide like an owl. I heard a faint sound of water and realized he was urinating.

So, here we were. Fear was now on the other hoof. He was mine—if I wanted him. But, would it bring justice for Cervida's male? Would it stop the killings? Was the sheriff really right, that it is what it is? And what did that really mean? That this human in front of me was destined to kill moose and I was destined to allow it to happen and be a victim of his destiny? That my actions had no effect on the future, that the impact of my time on earth was no more significant than the dust of the decomposing antlers in my dreams?

I looked at the human in front of me, shaking like a baby moose. My anger had filtered out into the wind. Revenge was no longer guiding my consciousness. A feeling of destiny filled me with clarity and peace. I inhaled slowly, then exhaled deeply. "It is what it is," I repeated to myself three times. I bowed my head in honor of all the herbivores in a carnivore world.

Then I charged.

WOLF

A Freedom Story

"FETCH!"

"Excuse me?"

"Fetch. Go get the stick and bring it back."

"Go get the stick? I don't want the stick. You want it, you go get it."

I was halfway through my training for the Wolf Protection Program. The Alaskan government was shooting wolves from the air again and a pack of us alpha wolves came up with a plan to save our species. We would train ourselves to behave as domestic dogs so we could be taken in by human packs where we would be protected until it was safe to go back into the wild. The program got off to a rough start when the alpha wolves fought for domination of the school. We finally agreed we had to compromise, which isn't easy for a pack of alpha wolves.

"Roll over and put your legs in the air."

"And expose my stomach?"

"Exactly."

"That doesn't work for me. I'm too dominant for that."

"Then, 'Sit.'"

"I am sitting."

"Then stand up and sit when I say so."

"Oooookay."

"Lie down and roll over."

"Oh, boy."

The concept of submission went against my very nature. To live in a human house as a dog sounded humiliating and defeating to me. I decided at an early age to be an alpha and, after many battles, I've never looked back.

We spent our mornings working on exercises in Speak, Sit, Roll Over and Bad Dog. The afternoons were more interesting. We studied the human language, in this case English. Languages come easy to me. I speak fluent Porcupine, Marmot and five Vole dialects. I can fake my way through Muskoxen and Caribou. English was easy. The conjugation of verbs and the present continuum tenses were simple enough for a moose to understand.

"Humans, by their body language and vocal tone, will usually tell you everything you need to know. However, there will be times when understanding English words will help in your disguise and may even save you. Especially if you hear the word 'vet,' or 'veterinarian.' Let's all say, 'veterinarian.'"

A veterinarian sounded great, taking care of the sick, but when our trainer explained spaying and neutering, the classroom exploded in howls.

"What?!"

"What kind of sickos are these humans?"

"I'd like to see them try that with me!"

"WHAT SHARP INCISORS AND CANINES YOU HAVE."

"The better to puncture, slash and cling to struggling prey," I said.

"What pointed premolars and molars you have."

"The better to shear and tear tendons and connective tissue," I said.

"What big back molars you have."

"The better to crack bones," I said.

A wolf in dentist's clothing was giving me my final medical checkup.

"Remember, we have the biting capacity of 1500 pounds per square inch," the dentist said, "twice that of a big dog like a German Shepherd. Humans have only a biting pressure of 300 pounds per square inch. As a domestic dog you will be given what the humans call toys, sometimes an animal bone. We can chew through a femur bone in six to eight bites. Don't. It will blow your cover. Play with the bone, gnaw on it, maybe leave some food."

"Leave some food?"

"ALL OF YOU ARE NOW MEMBERS OF THE ALPHA Canus Familiaris Force."

Our charismatic leader and head trainer, Loco Lobo, was giving us our graduation address. Every wolf pup in Alaska grew up hearing the adventures of Loco Lobo. He was missing a leg and he wore an eye patch over his right eye. He had chewed off his left hind leg when he was caught in a trap in Southeast Alaska. Part of his skull was blown off in an aerial assassination attempt that killed his alpha female domestic partner. Many pups played "Loco Lobo" together, limping and pretending they had only one eye.

"I don't have to tell anyone here the seriousness of our Alpha Force mission," Loco said, adjusting his eye patch with a front paw. "The goal of the humans to extirpate us from our range gets closer every year."

"Extirpate?"

"Yes, extirpate. Extinct means forever vanished from the planet. Extirpate means destroy or eliminate a species from an entire area within its range. It's a short pounce to extinction if we're wiped out here in Alaska. The War Against the Wolves is the longest war in the history of the world. The Greeks had bounties on us as early as 600 B.C. The last wolf was murdered in Denmark in 1772; Ireland—1821; Scotland—1848. By 1900, except for the Great Lakes region, wolves were gone from the eastern half of the United States. Between 1937 and 1969 federal agents massacred 52,000 of us in the western half of the United States. Even here in Alaska we were wiped out on the Kenai Peninsula by 1925. There may be as little as 7,000 wolves left in Alaska. Compare this to other species. In Alaska, there are 50,000 grizzly bears, over 100,000 black bears, and how about this? One million caribou. Am I the only wolf salivating over that?"

We all howled and laughed.

"But seriously. Over the last ten years over 1400 wolves have gone," Loco Lobo raised his front paws and squeezed them together over his head, " 'missing.' Why are they 'missing'? Traps, hunters and aerial attacks, that's why. The average wolf litter is four to seven pups, so, as the humans say, you do the math."

"In closing, as the elite Alpha Force, your mission is essential to our survival. As your leader I have one command I want you to always remember."

Loco Lobo paused, looked solemnly at us.

"Sit! Just kidding. Let's end with our secret Alpha Force howl."

Loco Lobo began with a simple howl. After a few seconds I started in with a howl, followed by another wolf, then another. Each of us wavered or modulated our howls, the different pitches creating a discordant sound that made it impossible to identify the pattern of a particular howler. Wolves call this the chorus howl. We use it so competing packs cannot tell how many of us wolves are around. Two wolves can make a choral sound that could be twenty wolves.

All of us were leaders from different packs. There had been many bloody, territorial battles, but we were now howling in unity. We thought our fights were wolf pack against wolf pack, but there was a deadlier foe than us.

I WAS ASSIGNED TO A LITTLE TOWN ON THE WATER A few hundred miles south from where I was born. A wolf travels at five miles an hour and covers up to 30 miles a day. I took my time, stopping to eat a marmot now and then, reflecting on the change in my life. In many ways I was excited. This was a challenge, something to achieve, a new world to conquer. On day five I reached the pass that lead down into the valley of my new home. I was surrounded by mountains and glaciers. I heard a river running in the distance. An eagle twittered above me.

Then I heard the plane.

I couldn't tell if it was an assassin plane, but it was coming fast and I was in open tundra, exposed. I broke into a run. The plane was above me quicker than a bird of prey. The sound of the first shot exploded in my ears. I shifted into high gear, taking evasive action. I wove back and forth so the killers couldn't get a straight shot at me. I heard the bullets flying by me. My lungs hurt. There was nowhere to hide, but the sound of a river was getting stronger, and I ran in that direction. I made a hard right turn and the plane had to circle to come back at me. That gave me some time between bullets.

I had been at full throttle for a few miles now and I felt a fatigue I wasn't familiar with. The sound of the river was stronger and I knew that was my chance of survival. A bullet hit a rock near me and echoed away. Another bullet exploded in the earth and dirt sprayed into my eyes, blinding me. I moved toward the sound of the water, shaking my head to clear the dirt out of my eyes. The plane was above me, rattling my brain with its engines, like a million wasp nests.

Though my vision was blurred, I could hear the river next to me and I jumped for the water. I felt a sharp burn in my hip as I hit the river and I knew I'd been shot. The current was strong and the water cold. My survival instinct overcame my pain. I wolf paddled down the river, the natural flow giving me a feeling of freedom. I came around a turn and I saw a partially submerged log blocking the river. One of the most dangerous objects in a river, I'd seen a beta wolf sucked under a log and drowned. I tried to swim to shore but the current was too strong. If I could approach the log straight on I could try to crawl over it, but my left hip wasn't working right and my coat was thick and heavy with water, like a moose carcass was smothering me.

My head slammed into the log and the force of water pushed me under. I popped out the other side, gasping for air. I looked down river and there was more debris. I bounced off stumps and was slapped by branches as I tried to find an eddy or the shore. Around the next turn was a beaver dam and I slammed right through the living room.

"Barry! There's a wolf in the house!"

I popped out the back of the dam and landed in an eddy. I crawled to shore and collapsed. A male beaver stuck his head out of the dam.

"Hey, this is a one time thing, isn't it?"

I SPENT A FEW DAYS LICKING MY WOUNDS. MY HEAD was sore and there were cuts all over my legs and back. However, my hip injury wasn't as serious as it felt. It looked like the bullet grazed me, taking part of my fur and skin with it. After a few days of licking, the pain subsided.

According to my WPS (Wolf Positioning System) I was twenty-six miles from my new home. My plan was to arrive at the house at dawn. I started into town at midnight, my leg a dull ache. The streets were empty and I paced down Main Street. I looked in the windows of the stores. At the corner of Second and Main I stopped in my wolf tracks. In the window hung a wolf pelt. I turned and vomited into the street. Across from me humans sat in a bar. I heard the sounds of "Wooooo!" and "Sweeeeeeeeet!" I composed myself.

It was spring and there was still snow on the ground. When I turned onto a side street near my house, I ran into my first domestic dogs, a brown Labrador and some long-haired mix. They yelled at me.

"Hey, this is our neighborhood. Get out of here. What do you think you're doing?"

I stopped, paused and looked them in the eye.

"Well, I'm thinking about kicking both your butts if you don't shut up."

The dogs stood closer together and pushed out their chests.

"Oh, yeah? Well, come on. You want some of us?"

I stepped forward slowly, head down, baring my teeth. I growled low, letting some saliva drip from my mouth. The dogs backed up.

"Uh, hey, okay, no problem. What the heck. Welcome to the neighborhood."

I continued on in the dark. The house was quiet when I located it. I lay down and waited. When morning light lit up the street I heard sounds from inside the house. I moved closer to the door. A young human boy opened the door, his eyes bugged out, and then he yelled:

"Mommy!"

I was in neutral position #1, lying down, head up, tongue out, panting. The mother and father came to the door. The little boy started toward me.

"Stop, son!" the father said, "looks like a wolf."

I rolled over on my back, paws in the air and wiggled around. I made the whine of an omega wolf.

"Oh, he's so cute, Bob," the mother said.

"Looks like a wolf, Jamie," Bob said, "I'm getting my gun."

I immediately deployed Response #A4. I had placed a stick close to me. I got up on all fours, put the stick in my mouth and trotted over to Bob, my tail high and wagging. They had taught us in training that winning over the dominant male was essential for success. I dropped the stick in front of Bob.

"Bob, he wants to play 'fetch,'" Jamie said. "How adorable."

I could feel Bob's uncertainty. I got as low to the ground as possible, my front legs spread out, my butt in the air. I whimpered, and then I barked. Bob picked up the stick and I stood up and faced the direction in which he was moving his arm. He threw the stick and I blew after it in a full sprint. He didn't have much of an arm and even with my hip injury I easily caught the stick before it hit the ground. I spun around and raced back to Bob, dropped the stick and flopped on my back and twisted from side to side.

"Oh, Bob," Jamie said, "we've been talking about getting a dog."

"Can we keep him?" the little boy said.

"GOOD DOG, KEVERY."

Kevery? That's me. I had a metal tag hanging from a rope around my neck that said, "Woof, my name is Kevery. I'm lost. Please call my mom Jamie @766-0000." As if I was a mentally challenged hybrid or that I had the brain capacity of a moose.

Lost.

I had been "domesticated" for two weeks. The family had fought over taking me in. Papa Bob said no way, Jamie begged, the child cried. Bob decided they would keep me for a month and see if anyone claimed me. However, Bob said I couldn't be in the house and had to sleep outdoors. What a relief.

Jamie was excited. She set up a bed on the porch. She brought me two kinds of food: a dry tasteless, pellet shaped substance and a mushy paste she took out of a can. She brought me a cow bone but I scared her when, not thinking, I chewed through it in a couple of bites.

My instinct, of course, was to roam and mark territory. My old pack had a range of 400 square miles. But whenever I felt the mood coming on, Jamie would come out and say, "Kevery, stay, good dog."

Bob was another story. He was mean. If he was in my pack I would handle him without a second thought, but I was out of my world now. At first I saw him as my biggest problem, but I came to see him as an opportunity for personal growth. I ignored him as much as possible, even when I listened to him speak.

Wolves are smart. Too smart. Things can bother us that shouldn't bother us. Having quickly mastered English in boot camp, it killed me to listen to Bob butcher his own language. Double negatives, blundering past participles, using "who" when he should be using "whom." Sometimes I had to slink off to a corner and silently howl to myself.

Yes, I was a good dog.

"YOU AIN'T NO DOG."

"Sure I am. Woof, woof."

"No, you're not."

"Why do you say that?"

"One, your paws are too big for your size. What do you weigh? 100 pounds?"

"So?"

"I've noticed your paw prints. They measure a good 4 ½ inches long by 3 ½ inches wide. Only huge dogs—way bigger than you—like Great Danes and St. Bernards, leave tracks larger than yours."

"Listen—"

"I'm not done, Wolfie. Wolves pace, dogs trot. I've watched you walking outside. You pace."

Her name was Princess. She looked like a lynx, but her paws were smaller and her legs longer. Instead of showing fear, Princess had ignored me since I joined the household. She was pushing my instincts.

"Where I come from, you'd be a meal right now," I said.

"Well, we're not where you come from, are we?" she said, lowering her head and raising her eyebrows.

I stood up. She raised her paw above her eyes and shook her body.

"Oh, no, a big bad wolf is coming to get me. What shall I do? Can my heart stand it?"

Princess lowered her paw, exhaled a breath and looked at me.

"Look, Wolfie, I'm not one of these lame dogs in the hood who run and hide when you bare your teeth and drool on the ground. I'm the Queen of this house and you better respect that."

"Or what?" I said. I made a quick move in her direction. She jumped from the porch to the top of Bob's truck. She did a little spin dance and exposed her butt to me and wiggled it at me. She was fast.

MY JOB WAS TO KEEP A LOW PROFILE, AND I WAS
determined to act submissive, but I had to burn my alpha energy. I
ran wind sprints up and down the yard to keep in shape. I was resting,
stretching, when I heard a small, female voice.

"Well, hello, big boy."

I looked over and there was a dog not much bigger than a squirrel. She
tapped her front paws excitedly on the ground.

"I heard there was fresh meat in town," she said. "Yahoo."

I stepped a few paces toward her.

"What are you?"

"What am I? Where you been? I am Chi-Chi the Chihuahua, baby, and
I'm thinking you and me should be seeing more of you and me."

"You're aggressive for a little dog."

"I'm not a little dog."

"Yes, you are."

"No, I'm not."

I squinted at the Chihuahua. She squinted back.

"I'm the same size you are, if not a little taller. You look about, from tip of
your nose to the tip of your tail to be six feet or so. Height at the shoulder
is about thirty inches. I'm just a little taller and longer. We're perfect. They
say for breeding the female should always be bigger."

"Breeding? You and me?"

"Try a Chihuahua, never go back."

"Who says that?"

"Everyone who's tried a Chihuahua."

A WOLF WITHOUT A PACK IS A LONE WOLF, AND A lone wolf is a lonely wolf. After a few weeks I would awaken in the middle of the night from the sound of a howl, only to find it was me. We wolves usually howl to find our companions or to keep our neighbors at bay. A wolf separated from his pack will find a common rendezvous site and howl for hours, waiting for his pack mates to respond. No one responded to my howls.

I was walking, after midnight, when I ran into her. She was circling the house where she lived. She had a bluish-white coat. Even in the dark, with my night vision, I could see she had one blue eye and one brown eye.

"Australian Shepherd," I said to her, recalling Dog Breeds and Tendencies from boot camp, "Cattle dog. Likes to circle and herd."

"Wow, throw the dog a bone," she said, not looking at me.

I followed as she circled her house again.

"What are you doing up this late at night?" I asked.

"Circling."

"Want to practice herding me?"

"Clever."

"Are you curious why I'm up late at night?"

"No, but I'm sure I know why you're sniffing around, but you're too early and you're also too late."

"What does that mean?"

"If you're so smart, why don't you figure it out," she said.

THERE WAS A STIR IN THE NEIGHBORHOOD. ALL THE male dogs were leaping up and down. It was a party. I went over to the pack standing in the middle of the street.

"What's going on?" I said.

"What's going on, he asks?" a Golden Retriever said.

"This is the start of the 30-day countdown to the Breeder's Race."

"Breeder's Race?"

"Only comes but twice a year, my fellow canine."

There are a few differences in breeding between dogs and wolves. A female dog reaches sexual maturity at six to eight months whereas a female wolf begins to procreate at two to four years old. Wolves only mate once a year, usually in February or March. Dogs mate twice a year.

"What are the rules?" I asked.

"Rules? There are no rules. Every dog to himself."

"Well, oh, look what we have here," said a part Basset hound, part Golden Retriever.

I looked over and saw the Australian Shepherd with another Shepherd. They were both on leashes, a woman walking them down the sidewalk.

"Oh, Sheila, Miss Purebred and her Tundra from Down Under."

The male walking with her gave the pack of us an Alpha stare. Oh, really, I thought to myself.

"The race just heated up," I said. The dogs looked at me eyeing Sheila.

"Watch it, Wolf, she ain't in the race."

"What do you mean?

"I mean, she don't mess with our class."

Class? Was there a caste system within the domestic dog world I should be aware of? I watched her walk. I let out a little growl under my breath. The male shepherd turned and looked at me.

"Mate, watch yer mouth there. Know your place or I'll put you in your place," he barked.

"Ooooooooooooooooh," the other dogs said in response to the challenge.

I smiled. A weak wolf barks; a strong wolf bites.

LATER THAT NIGHT I WAS ON MY WAY TO SHEILA'S
house when the Chihuahua appeared in front of me.

"Oh, no, it appears as if I dropped my bone and I just can't seem to reach it."

She stretched in front of me, lifting her tail and pushing her rump
in my face.

"Would be so nice if a big strong male would fetch me a bone."

"Not tonight, Ms. Chihuahua."

"You saying the name wrong. After you try a Chihuahua, you say,
'Gee, Wow, Wow.'"

I kept pacing past her. She yelled at me.

"Fetch, big boy! Fetch!"

I found Sheila lying on the ground, picking at her paw. There was blood
on her fur.

"Are you okay?"

"I'm great. I'm picking glass out of my pads and I'm bleeding all over my
coat. It's a dog's life and I love it."

"What happened?"

"Oh, those stupid young humans. They throw their beer bottles out of
the car window when they drive by. It makes me crazy. I feel like chasing
their cars like the other idiot dogs in the neighborhood do."

I leaned toward her and pushed her face away from her paw.

"Let me have a look at that."

I ran my tongue through her pads, checking for glass.

"Hey, watch it."

"Relax, I know what I'm doing," I said as licked her paw.

"Listen, if you think you can just trot over here and start...ooooooh...licking
my...well, you do know what you're doing...hmmm...that feels good."

She suddenly stood up, flustered.

"I should...I have some...I need to circle..."

"Sit down. You need to let those cuts heal."

Sheila sat down. She looked at me, then looked away. I moved closer to her.

"I better check your face for glass," I said, as I licked her nose.

"Hey, what we got here?"

The male I had seen her walking with was in front of us. Primal instincts raced through my nervous system. Sheila jumped up, stumbled when she put pressure on her injured paw.

"It's not what it looks like. He was just...this is...I don't know your name..."

"I don't care who he is. He's not long for this world is what he is. But I'll tell you who I am. I'm her mate, mate, and she only mates with me, not some lowlife like you."

Ears back, hair up, saliva began to drip from my mouth. Sheila backed away. I didn't move. He walked up and growled in my face.

"Want to have a go at it?"

I moved faster than he could think. I bit his jaw and pushed him to the ground. He wrestled with me but I turned him over and bit his rump and then his back legs. He let out a loud yelp. Then I sunk my teeth deep in his neck and pushed him down. He whimpered and whined, the signs of defeat.

The door to Sheila's house opened and a woman ran screaming at me.

"He's killing our little Dundee! Oh, my...get your gun Larry!"

I knew about guns. I let go of Dundee and ran back to my house. I heard the phone ring inside the house as I moved to my bed. The door burst open and Bob moved quickly toward me.

"Bob, he's a good dog."

I could feel Bob's aggression and with my adrenal high it was hard to play dog. But I faced him and wagged my tail. He kicked me in the stomach and slapped the side of my head. He dragged me by my neck to a tree.

"I told you we should have fixed him and now we will," Bob said, his hands doing something with my collar.

Fixed? A rush of icy river water ran through my blood.

"The vet only comes to town once a month," Jamie said.

"Well, find out when or I'll do it myself."

I looked at Bob and thought how with one bite I could fix him. Bob walked over and stood by the door and watched me as he and Jamie talked. With the vet coming the mission was now aborted. I wondered how the rest of my brothers were doing out there. For me, it was time to go home. Now. I took a breath, looked around and sprinted for the street. Watch me, Bob, my rear end the last thing you see of me. When I reached full speed I felt I hit a wall of trees, my throat constricted. I fell, trying to suck up breath. Was I shot? I tried to move again but my head snapped backward. I looked behind me. Some type of rope was attached to my collar.

A wave of nausea bubbled up from my stomach and crested in my throat. I stood up on my hind legs and pushed forward, testing the restraint gently, as if there had been a mistake. My collar pulled on me like a tight mouth. I looked behind me. The rope was secured around a big cottonwood tree.

I figured I could chew through it quickly and gain back my freedom. I sunk my teeth into the line, feeling for the weak point. There was no give, like I was biting into rock. I chewed along the rope, looking for an opening. I went to the tree and began tugging at the rope, trying to break it free of the trunk. Although it was mid-day, a sense of darkness draped over me, as if I was surrounded by a rival wolf pack. I shook off the feeling. I looked at the mountains and took off at full speed, the rope loose behind me. I ran with confidence. At full throttle I felt the rope tighten and I was slammed back as if by powerful winds. I gasped for breath, ran back to the tree and sprinted again. The rope ripped me to the ground. I ran back and repeated my escape attempt and my body snapped back hard to the earth. I tore at the rope. Using my paws, I tried to push the collar over my ears. I rolled in the dirt, using all four legs to try to free the yoke around my neck. I ran around the tree, trying every angle to loosen the rope grip on the trunk.

"Bob, please do something. He'll kill himself," Jamie said from somewhere far away.

"He'll learn, honey, he'll learn."

Little Bobby cried.

I took a deep breath and sprinted toward the mountains with its forest of trees. At the peak of my run the tautness of the rope spun me around. I ran again and again, racing faster and faster. Each time the rope ripped me harder to the ground. Pain howled from my neck to my tail. Breath rattled from my throat as I pushed myself up slowly from each rejection. On one final sprint a fire raged through my body when I hit the earth. Something popped in my rib cage. I tried to get up but I could only lift my head and stare out at the mountains. I vomited on the ground. Before I passed out, the last thing I saw were the river channels of blood flowing through my vomit.

"I'LL HUFF AND I'LL PUFF AND I'LL BLOW YOUR HOUSE DOWN."
I am surrounded by houses full of pigs. The houses are pressed together like trees in a dense forest. Thin rays of light peak through the cracks between the houses.

I have an idea. I'll blow a few of the houses down and that will open an escape route for me. I should have time to eat a pig or two as well.

I push my chest out as I inhale but when I blow nothing comes out but a weak cough. I try again but my exhale is even weaker. I sink lower on each attempt until I collapse like a fallen bird. I hear the pigs laughing in the houses.

"Ooooh, what a big, bad wolf! Scarrrrry!"

I WAKE UP AND LOOK AT THE MOUNTAINS ABOVE THE town. I instinctively jump up and try to escape. The chain stops me. I turn around and start chewing on the line, but, of course, my teeth don't make a dent.

"Lose your teeth doing that, Wolfie."

Princess the cat strolls over to me.

"This thing is made of metal. No way you chew through that."

Princess stops and looks at me, then starts cleaning her face.

"Look, we didn't get off on the right paw. I have territorial issues. But this tying you up isn't right. Humans been tying up creatures for centuries. Even their own species. A couple of million tied up in this country alone. Think it's going to make everyone safe. What's safe?"

Princess stopped and licked herself for another minute.

"I see where they're serving you slop-in-a-bowl. Can I get you anything? A mouse, a vole? Free range. A bird or two?"

I shook my head.

"Not a big bird fan. Too many bones, all those feathers."

"Who's the princess now?"

Princess started to walk away.

"I'm sorry. No creature deserves to have its freedom stolen."

FEAR.

I have seen fear in the eyes of a moose. In the eyes of a caribou. In the eyes of another wolf. Have I known fear? I've certainly known danger. It was danger that drove us into the Wolf Protection Program. Facing your danger: taking what appears to be an uncontrollable situation and controlling that situation with strength, patience and intelligence.

So do I have fear now that I have failed at controlling my danger? Do I have a fear of death? A fear of captivity? And ironically, I am in a town surrounded by creatures that have a fear of freedom, who appear to be madly in love with what they fear.

And here I lay, strapped to a tree by a chain made from unnatural material waiting for a human to come and maim me so I will be a tame animal and everyone will feel safe and that will give them freedom...from what?

I suppose the humans could make the case that what has happened to me is what I have done to so many wolves over the years—dominated and made them submit. But really the alpha wolf is the leader, who, by determining everyone's role, sets up the pack for success. We are a team and each member knows what is expected of them.

And what role is expected of me in my submission? That I will no longer roam? That I will fetch on command? That I will roll over and play dead like a good doggie?

Am I afraid? Of what? I am no longer who I was. I am defeated. I am an alpha wolf no more. What is there to fear?

"HI."

I look into one blue and one brown eye.

"How are you?"

I shrug.

"I feel terrible. I feel it's my fault that you're in your situation."

"Your fault because your left eye has the deep blueness of glacial ice and your right eye has the rich texture of cottonwood bark? Your fault because your fur has the sheen and softness of low alpine heather? Your fault because when you walk you sway like spring flowers in a soft wind?"

"Well..." Sheila said, looking away. "I...ah...you have a way with words."

"I have a way with the truth."

Sheila lay down next to me and we sat in silence as the sun began its descent.

"What's it like out there?" Sheila asked.

I pulled at the collar, looked at the chain that held me and gave out a short laugh.

"Free. Unpredictable. Challenging. Sometimes you don't have food for days, but you never think you won't survive. Knowing everything will be all right, that there will be enough abundance, that's freedom."

"I want to know what it's like to be free," Sheila said, moving closer to me.

"Freedom comes with risks and consequences."

"And not seeking freedom doesn't?"

"It doesn't come with risks."

"I've never taken a risk."

"Why take one now?"

Sheila turned her head and licked her fur a few times, paused and picked at something between the pads of her right paw.

"I've always been taken care of. Fed, petted, brushed. But there was always a bit of unhappiness and unfulfilled ambition that nipped at me like a flea. Ever since I was a little puppy girl I ran in circles. I thought the circling was an expression of my herding instincts, but now I know it was a symbol of being stuck in a cycle and I couldn't find an exit. And the incidents of the last few days have opened my eyes and showed me a possible escape from the circle."

"Escape to where?"

Sheila stood up and moved closer to me.

"Wherever you're going?"

I tugged on my collar and rattled my chains.

"Look like I'm going anywhere?"

Sheila noticed something and leaned in for a closer look. Her mouth was almost touching mine. The smell of her rich dog breath both comforted me and excited me.

"You have some blood on your mouth," she said, as she leaned forward.

"Hey! Get out of here!"

Sheila jumped and shuffled her feet, her tail between her legs. Bob came waddling across the yard. He hurled a ball that hit Sheila in the side. She yelped and ran off.

"You don't have to throw things at her," I barked at Bob.

Bob walked over to me.

"You talking to me, smart dog?"

I inhaled deeply, shook my head and exhaled. Who else would I be talking to Bob? Do you see any other idiots throwing objects at dogs for no reason?

"Two days."

Bob used two of his fingers in a cross motion.

"Then snip snip. Snip, snip."

"I GOT PEE ALL INSIDE MY TRUCK!"

I woke up. Bob slammed his door and looked around, first at me, then toward the other suspects in the neighborhood. Sheila sat across the street. When our eyes met she wagged her tail.

The local pack was hanging out further up the street, running their mouths, as usual.

"Not like we haven't had our share of violence in our neighborhood. Remember when you ate Pekinese Pete?"

"Don't start. You don't know what it's like living with a Pekinese."

"And I'm not judging. I liked Pete—"

"You didn't know Pete."

"I knew Pete on a secondary level. You had a primary relationship with him. I understand that. What I'm saying is—"

"Enough, you two. Pete's dead. It was his time."

"Oh, no, here we go. Mr. New Age, O Great Flea Whisperer. 'It was his time.' What's time to a dog?"

"I'm sorry you're too shallow to understand."

"I'm not shallow. I'm deaf due to your daily meditations, the eardrum shattering peal you create playing your Sacred Canine Singing Food Bowls with your nails."

"I wish you could step inside my fur and listen to you bark all day. Is there anything that doesn't make you bark? You bark when the wind blows. It's like living next door to a 24 hour All-Bark Radio station."

"What? Sorry, can't hear you. I have a Sacred Canine Singing Food Bowl ringing in my ear."

"The bowls create a sound similar to the function of the chorus howl of wolves, our ancient ancestors who—"

"Segue. If I may interrupt this Meeting of the Mutts. Our local wolf."

"He should get a bone for putting that pompous herd dog in his place."

"And, instead, he's getting...fixed... tomorrow."

"Fixed. Right."

"No, wrong. Domesticated. Disempowered."

"What are you calling me?"

"We are born into our domestic world and there are rules that are put upon us. The wolf is not of our world and he is only visiting our world."

"And what can we do about it?"

"We're not as disempowered as they think we are. Sheila has a plan."

Bob started up the truck and the voices were lost in the sound of the engine.

"THE FERRY'S COMING! THE FERRY'S COMING!" THE chocolate lab barked the news as he ran up from the harbor. Sheila nodded and the neighborhood gang took off toward the house and where Princess lay. Princess, on cue, ran to the spruce tree and scratched her way up high in the limbs. The dogs jumped on the trunk, all of them giving a strong dog howl, staring up at Princess.

The door opened and Jamie ran out, exhaled at the sight and put her hand to her mouth.

"Bob!"

Bob ran out, yelled at the dogs until they ran away. Then Princess began to meow.

"You're going to have to get her, Bob, remember what happened last time," Jamie said.

"She'll come down when she's hungry," Bob said, moving back to the house.

Princess went to a full scream. I covered my ears with my paws. She raised the pitch higher, windows in nearby houses bending with the sound. Neighbors came out, pained looks on their faces. Bob came out of the house, cursing, went behind the house and grabbed a ladder and carried it to the tree.

Sheila and Chi-Chi ran to me.

"Okay, we don't have much time. We can't chew through the rope but the collar is leather and we can chew through that."

The Chihuahua stared at my collar.

"I like a male in leather."

"Enough, Chi-Chi," Sheila said as she examined my constraints.

"You talking to me, girl? Careful how you talk to a dog of my pedigree."

"Cut the trashy rat dog talk and get to work."

"Excuse me, b—"

Sheila turned to Chi-Chi. An alpha growl came out of her.

"Beautiful. Excuse me, beautiful, is what I was going to say."

The two females went to work on my collar, tearing at the leather. Princess's wails continued to pierce the air. We all looked up and saw Bob in the tree now, reaching for Princess as she backed away from him, higher into the tree. Chi-Chi tore back into her mission, shaking the collar like it was a carcass.

"We're almost there," Sheila said, spitting bits of leather out the side of her mouth.

"I liiiiike it," Chi-Chi growled, ripping deeper into the collar.

"Oh, no," Sheila said, feeling resistance. "There's a wired lining inside the leather...and there's Bob."

We looked up and Bob had noticed us. He was descending the ladder quickly. When he was halfway down the Lab ran under the ladder and knocked it over, tumbling Bob to the ground.

"We have to figure out a way," Sheila said, then looked at me. "No, freedom. I know we'll figure out a way."

The smell of a human froze all of us. Jamie reached toward me. Chi-Chi and Sheila bared their teeth and growled at her. Jamie stopped.

"It's okay girls, it's okay."

Jamie unlatched the rope, then undid the buckle on the collar and removed it. She petted me on the head. I stood up, my legs weak from days of inactivity. I looked at Jamie, her hand resting on my head.

"You've got to go now, Kevery."

I licked her hand and wagged my tail at her. Why not?

Then I ran.

THERE'S A DIFFERENCE BETWEEN RUNNING AWAY AND running toward. There's a difference between escaping from and escaping to. There's a difference between avoiding the dark and embracing the light.

The oxygen in the air fueled me straight to my bloodstream, each breath pulling me deeper toward the wilderness. Sheila was running behind me as we left the town, cut across the Chilkat River flats and headed up the center of the valley.

"Wheeeee! Woof, woof!" she yelled as we raced along.

When we reached the banks of the Klehini River we stopped and rested in the beds of fluffy horsetail grass. We rolled and played and tossed through the foliage. We stopped to catch our breath.

"I'm hungry," she said. "Is there a special tonight?"

"It's not a bowl of mud served out of a can or a bowl of dried pellets that looks and probably tastes like rat scat."

"Surprise me."

I paused, looked down and tossed some dirt away with my paw. The sun was sneaking behind the mountains.

"Sheila, sometimes we wolves don't eat for days. You've been raised with regular feeding times and measured amounts of food. When we get a kill we can eat up to 20 pounds of meat because we don't know when we'll eat again."

Sheila looked around at the last flashes of day.

"I'm cold," she said, a soft revelation shining in her blue eye.

"Come here," I said, as I raised my front leg and she curled underneath me.

"No funny stuff, Mr. Wolf. I ain't that type of dog. I ain't no Chihuahua."

I licked her nose and softly howled in her ear as we snuggled together. The light from the moon lit up our coats. I feel asleep to the soft sound of the wagging of her tail as it slapped against me.

I WOKE UP TO THE SIGHT OF SHEILA GROOMING herself a few feet away from me, licking herself clean. She noticed me and, a little embarrassed, she composed herself and walked over.

"Thank you for being in my world," she said.

"Thank you for being in my world."

Sheila looked around the huge expanse of the valley.

"I'm going back to my world where I'm comfortable and safe," she said.

"And I'm home now where I'm comfortable and safe."

Sheila tightened her mouth, smiled at me and turned and headed back to town. I watched her for a few minutes before I began my journey up valley.

I walked and ran and when I was near the pass I heard the sound and the plane passed over head. While the plane began to circle back I looked down at the river and over at a stand of trees, both possible safe zones for me. I chose the exposed, softly rolling flatland exploding with wild flowers.

"Show me what you got! Show me what you got!" I barked at the plane as it started toward me.

My paws tore at the earth as I started my run. The mixture of wildflowers and decay filled my nose. The buzz of the plane shook my eardrums. My lungs expanded as I ran, hard and fast, no collar, no leash, no rope. I am an alpha wolf. I am strong. I am fearless.

I am free.

EAGLE

A Commitment Story

LIKE MOST SUB-ADULT MALES, I COULDN'T WAIT TO mate, but, like most sub-adult males, I did more waiting than mating. Just before my 5th birthday, when my head and tail turned as white as the Cathedral Peaks, I hit the eagle bars.

My first try was a wild roost in Skagway called the Gestation Station. I auditioned, often but unsuccessfully, for the Mating Game, a weekly contest where a female with a blanket over her head chose from among a perch of male eagles after asking them silly questions.

My next stab was the Talon Lock, a bar down by the Haines airport. It wasn't much to look at—gravel on the floor, driftwood for stools, salmon skulls lying around the joint. And the Lock, as it was called, wasn't great for meeting females, either. The place could get rough. One night some ravens came in and me and the fellas had to stomp them.

Out of desperation I even joined a mating service called Soar and Score, but it turned out to be a multi-level marketing scam set up by eagles from California.

Then I discovered the Breed and Brood, a classy club located in the Council Grounds Complex, a thick stand of cottonwoods in the center of the Bald Eagle Preserve. The Brood had a contemporary debris décor—tin cans, Styrofoam cups, plastic bottles. The B & B was known to have the best entertainment in the valley, featuring a female a cappella group, the Aves Marias. A comedian was on limb the night I met Leu.

"What do you call an osprey living in a valley of eagles?" he asked the crowd.

"What?" an eagle chittered from the back.

"Hungry," said the comedian.

The crowd went cuckoo, flapping their wings, banging their tails on branches.

"Why did they want the turkey as the national symbol instead of us?"

"I give up, why?" an eagle perched up front said.

"Because turkeys are easier to shoot."

Flapping of wings, banging of tails.

Then Leu flew in and knocked me off my perch. She had big yellow eyes, nice plumage, sharp talons. She bounced over to the other side of my limb.

"Is this branch taken?" she asked sweetly.

"Uh...uh...uh...no," I stuttered, a woodpecker attacking my heart.

"I'm Leu," she said.

"I'm Hal."

I was finishing the Brood's dinner special—spawned salmon tartar. The fish was aged to perfection with just a hint of early parasite infestation. She looked down at my meal, held tightly between my talons.

"Did you know that a salmon has 79% eatable flesh, whereas a duck only has 68% eatable flesh?" she said.

"Well, no...I mean...yeah, I knew that."

Not only was she pretty, she was smart, too. She was raised in Juneau, she said, and she had just finished her studies as a Stalmaster Scholar at the coveted Raptor Center in Sitka. She pointed to objects a mile away and told me about the number of light sensitive cells, or photoreceptors, which determine the detail of vision for an eagle. We have 1 million per square millimeter of retina, she said, where tourists have 200,000.

Did I know, she asked, that our vision is three to four times greater than tourists and that we have both monocular and binocular visions? Or, that we perceive five basic colors, allowing us to see subtle tones and to pick out prey hiding in grass and brush?

I was mesmerized, molting at every word. We perched there for hours. The owner of the Brood interrupted us while Leu was explaining the different caloric counts between one hour of flapping and one hour of soaring and gliding (161 to 47).

"You two building a nest? We're closed. Scram."

I invited her down to the pier at Fort Seward in front of the little red building that used to be the telegraph office during the War Against the Eagles. We sat on the pilings and looked out at the water. A whale breeched in the middle of the Lynn Canal. I turned to Leu.

"Hungry? I'll go grab that sucker with my talons."

"Oh, stop," she said, placing her left wing over her bill to hide a giggle.

We talked and talked, opening up to each other. I confessed my fear of losing my feathers. She asked me if I thought she was fat. She felt she was putting on weight and had decided to consume less than six percent of her body weight each day as opposed to the average eagle's consumption of seven to twelve percent of its body weight.

During a pause in our conversation, I gently preened her feathers and pecked at her bill. She lowered her head, spread her wings and let out a soft, high-pitched note.

"Nice vocal display," I said.

"Thank you very much."

For the next few weeks I chased her through the sky. Talons touching, we practiced rolling together as we exchanged positions. Then, on a Thursday night at the Gestation Station, we won the Cartwheel Display when we performed a complicated, innovative dive highlighted by triple axle spins and whirls.

We talked about honeymooning in Glacier Bay, shopping for a nest site. Kids.

I FLEW DOWN TO THE ROOST TO SEE MY BUDDIES. WE exchanged the traditional eagle greeting.

"Ya all right?"

"Pretty good, ya all right?"

"I'm all right, uh huh, I'm okay."

The whole gang was there. Fovea Joe was originally from down south but he flew up one summer and decided to stay. Old Man Canus, close to 40-years-old, was constantly picking up garbage and trying to find a use for it. Crazy Clo was, well, crazy as a loon. He suffered from Enumerative Plumage Syndrome, an obsessive disorder where an eagle constantly counts his 7,182 feathers. Not much is known about EPS, but Leu told me they think the disease is triggered by stress. The rumor in the roost had it that Clo began his downward spiral into feather counting after the love of his life flew south.

"Morning, Hal," Fovea Joe said, "you seem to be flying high today."

"Sure am," I said.

"2,162, 2,163, 2,164..." Clo counted off in his corner of the cottonwood.

"What gives, Hal?" Canus said, working on a tin can he found on the Haines Highway.

"Well, fellas, I've found a mate," I said proudly.

Canus looked up from his tin can. Clo stopped counting. Fovea Joe rubbed his beak.

"You mean mate as in nest, screaming eaglets 24 hours a day?" Fovea Joe said.

"As in mate FOR LIFE?" Canus said.

"Uh, yeah," I said.

"What do you know about her?"

"Well, she's smart, loving, considerate."

"Hah!" Fovea Joe said. "That'll last one season, max."

"Million to one it will work," Clo said.

"Have you met her mother?" Canus squawked at me.

"Her mother?" I said, a thin layer of storm clouds forming in the back of my brain.

"Yes, her mother. Got to meet her mother. That's what she'll be in five years. Her mother's a vulture, you better catch the first thermal out of there."

"Seen it a thousand times," Clo said.

"You don't want to limit your choices, Hal," Fovea Joe said. "What if someone better comes along? Happened to a good friend of mine. Nothing he could do, being mated for life and all. Never see him."

"She sounds suspicious to me," Canus said, "a little too good to be true. I haven't even met her and I can tell you she has more problems than a raven has tricks."

"Never build a nest with someone who has more troubles than you," Fovea Joe said.

"You got that right," Canus said.

"Say goodbye to Thursday night at the Gestation Station."

"So long to the Talon Lock."

"Bye-bye Breed and Brood."

"WAAAAAAAAAH! WAAAAAAAAAH!"

Leu and I were in our nest. Our two children, daughter Emma, son Juvie, were wailing for food. Leu, quite a bit heavier than when we first met, was stomping around.

"We need a fish every three hours for two chicks, Hal. Let's go!"

"Waaaaaaaaah! Waaaaaaaaah!"

"C'mon, Hal, if you can't handle this, what are you going to do when they're almost grown and need two pounds at each meal?"

I felt as if a trumpeter swan was stuck in my skull. There were strings attached to my wings pulling me far, far away.

"Aiiiieeeee!"

I woke up screaming. I'd been snoozing on a cottonwood near where the Tsirku River feeds into the Chilkat. A raft full of tourists was taking my picture.

"DID YOU FORGET ABOUT OUR APPOINTMENT?"

"Our appointment?"

"Hello? The tree realtor is dropping by to show us some nest sites."

"Oh...right, right."

"Are you okay, Hal?"

"Me? Fine, Leu, great."

"Would you like to do a little Cartwheel Display before we look at trees?"

"I'd love to, but gee, you know, I have this headache that's killing me."

"Hal?"

"Yeeeah?"

"What's going on?"

"Uh...nothing...I mean, not really...you know...everything's fine...sort of...not really, but you know...that's okay...everything's great."

"Hal?"

"Well, it's sort of...let me see...things seem to be moving kind of quickly...you know...and I thought...you being so smart and stuff...that you would think...a..."

"Think what, Hal?"

"Oh...you know, how fast things are going...how we really don't know each other that well...geez, I've never even met your mother..."

"We're not mating, is that what you're telling me?"

"Well, no. I mean yes. Not right now. But I still want to see you."

"Goodbye, Hal."

"You're not upset, are you, Leu?"

"Why would I be upset, Hal, since I'm so smart. And stuff."

"I'll call you."

"Don't bother."

FOR THE NEXT TWO WEEKS I SPENT DAY AND NIGHT IN the bars, celebrating my freedom. However, something happened one night at the Gestation Station while I was leading the crowd in a rousing rendition of "99 Tails of Trout on the Shore."

Between the 59th and 60th tail a wave of stupidity and loss blew over me. I ruffled the feeling away. I was having too much fun.

Then at the Talon Lock I started a driftwood clearing brawl when I clarified for the crowd a distinction that Leu had taught me—that the robin was actually the national bird and the bald eagle was the national symbol.

"What kind of carrion you trying to feed us, boy?" a big, burly eagle said to me.

"Yeah. What kind of dodo bird told you that one?" said another.

"She's no dodo bird, okay?" I said, heating up. "If there are any dodo birds around here, I'm looking at them."

Wings were flapped, beaks were exchanged, talons were locked.

Feathers flew.

And things weren't going so well at the Breed and Brood, either. I had carved in the gravel a detailed map to help explain Bergmann's Rule (members of warm-blooded species tend to be larger in the cooler parts of the breeding range, helping to preserve their body heat). My date stared at me and said, "Huh?"

I thought I was clicking with this one cutie so I invited her down to the pier to watch the whales.

"Hungry? I'll go grab one of those orcas for you."

"They're too big," she said. "I don't think you can lift it."

"4,442, 4,443, 4,444..."

"Afternoon, Hal," Fovea Joe said. "You seem to be flying kind of low today."

"I'm flying fine," I said defensively.

"Whatever."

"Not whatever. I'm flying fine," I said, my feathers ruffling slightly.

"4,661, 4,662, 4,663..." Clo droned on in the background.

"Whoa, time out," Fovea Joe said, walking over to me. "You can't scavenge a scavenger, Hal. What's the problem?"

"You got that right," Canus said, playing with a bread bag he had picked up from a tourist luncheon. "You can't scavenge a scavenger."

"5,001, 5,002, 5,003..."

"Still miss that female, huh?" Fovea Joe said.

"Yeah, I suppose."

"It'll pass. Come on, hang out with us for awhile. We'll cheer you up."

I looked over at Clo.

"5,298, 5,299, 5,300..."

I looked over at Canus. He was dragging a piece of webbing from the river. I turned to Fovea Joe.

"I don't think so."

I took off down the Chilkat Valley, caught a thermal, dipped over the range into Chilkoot Lake, flew down to Haines and back up the Chilkat River. I spied a salmon, a four-pounder or so, working his way up a thin channel near where the Tsirku River meets the Chilkat. I dove, leveled off near the water and snatched the salmon right at the tail. Yes, perfect, I thought as I lifted off. However, the salmon tossed and twisted and as I gained momentum I lost my grip and the fish tumbled to the water, disappearing in a deeper channel.

I was losing my touch.

I KNEW I'D FIND LEU DOWN ON THE LOWER DELTA OF the Tsirku conducting one of her science experiments. I landed beside her.

"Hello, Leu."

"Hello," she said, her tone an icy wind blowing out of Skagway.

"What ya doing?"

"Counting. I'm disturbed by the disproportion of Sockeye coming back to spawn and the corresponding smolt going out to sea."

"Hmmm, fascinating," I said.

We sat in silence while she worked. I drummed a talon on a tree trunk that had washed up on the gravel bar.

"Ah...I've been thinking, Leu...uh...I think I'm ready to mate."

"Really?"

"Really."

"Have you found a victim yet?"

"Very funny," I said. "I thought, you know, we could try it again."

"Well, you're thinking, Hal, and that's good. But you're thinking wrong, and that's bad."

Some type of sea eagle landed between us. Leu perked up.

"I'm sorry I'm late, Leu-Leu," the eagle said with a regional accent I wasn't familiar with. He pecked her on both sides of the face. "Just the thought of seeing you wreaks havoc with my regulated heterothermy, fluctuating my body temperature way beyond the narrow range of an eagle."

"Oh, Aquilo," Leu said, giggling.

Aquilo?

"Leu-Leu," he continued, "the cones and rods of your beautiful yellow eyes illuminate me and bring depth and perception to my life."

"Oh, Aquilo," Leu said again.

"Excuse me," I said, hacking a few times, "there must be some DDT residue drifting up from down south because it's getting pretty thick around here."

They ignored me. I lifted off, an invisible log dragging my heart down into the river.

"Leu-Leu, I know they say that male and female eagle plumages are the same, but there are those of us who are monomorphic, then there is you. Nature pays homage to your plumage; rivers choke with spawning salmon and lakes overflow with baby ducks."

"Oh, Aquilo."

I WASN'T HAPPY. AND IF I WASN'T HAPPY, NOBODY was going to be happy.

I came up behind an arctic tern and whacked him with a body slam. I swooped down and scattered a couple of crows snacking on a fish on a gravel bar. Flying over a raft full of tourists, I posed for their photos, and then I laid some droppings on them.

Down by where the Chilkat flows into the Lynn Canal a sea otter was swimming on its back, a little baby trout in its paws. Doubling behind the otter's head so he couldn't see me, I dropped down behind him, skimmed across the water and snatched the fish out of his hands.

"Hey!" the otter yelled at me, "you stole my fish!"

I circled above him, the fish flopping back and forth in my talons.

"Give me back my fish, you kleptoparasite!" he fussed, slapping the water.

"Such language," I said calmly, circling lower, dangling the fish just out of his reach.

"GIVE ME BACK MY FISH, YOU OVERRATED, SCAVENGING VULTURE!"

"I'd love to stay but I'm starving."

I leaned to the right, caught the wind and headed up river, the otter's curses fading in the distance.

EAGLES DON'T JUST STEAL FROM OTHER ANIMALS. WE rob from each other as well. We don't advertise this trait since we are the national symbol and all.

However, the word "stealing" was never uttered in our nest while I was growing up. My mother called it "displacement."

"Crows steal, ravens steal," she would say while she ripped bits of flesh from a flopping salmon. "We displace."

Right, Mom.

This is how it works. An eagle catches a fish and starts to eat it. Eagles land nearby, waiting for an opportunity to "displace" him. One eagle will take the initiative and flap, shove, beak or talon wrestle the first eagle out of the way. Well, it wasn't going to happen today.

Two big, dumb Yukon eagles landed near me while I ate my little trout.

"Hey, Waldo, what say we have us a bite to eat?"

"I could stand a kilogram or two, Dorp."

I looked over at them and stopped eating. I covered the food with my wings.

"Listen up, my mentally challenged falconiformes. I am going to talk reeeeeal slow so you don't have a problem understanding. You make one move toward my lunch and I will pull your third eyelid down over your bill, then I will carve tic-tac-toe on your throat with my talons. Are our voices on the same frequency?"

The two Canadian eagles looked at each other.

"Eh, we're eagles. We steal from each other. You trying to mess with nature?"

"No, dumbos, nature's trying to mess with me. Scram, go home."

I flapped my wings at them and they took flight, bumped into each other, and then flew in circles. They landed back in the same spot. I gave them the stink eye.

"Uh, sorry, but uh, eh, which way is north?"

"HOW DO YOU SAVE A BOATLOAD OF DROWNING pesticide salesmen?"

"HOW?" the eagle crowd crowed.

"Who cares?"

The Breed and Brood audience let out a collective "oooooh" followed by laughter.

"What do you call two Spotted Owls in the same forest?"

"WHAT?"

"History."

Wings flapped and tails banged.

I was sitting on a branch at the Brood, one wing draped over a twig. I was cocky from anger and rejection. A pretty female, quite a bit larger than me, landed close by.

"Nice wing primaries," I said.

"Flap off," she said, not even looking at me.

"What's your problem, hon? You wake up on the endangered list?"

"I'm not your hon," she said, turning her neck 270 degrees to face me. Her feathers went back.

"Hal? Is that you? It's me, Cece, your third cousin, fourth time removed. Stop flirting with me. You look awful. Get some help."

An immature female landed on a limb above me. A pretty girl, she couldn't have been more than four-years-old. Her eyes were still creamy, her beak gray and yellow, her head gray and light brown, her lower breast brown with some gray, her wing tips mottling gray, her tail gray with black.

"Buy me a salmon?" she said, trying to be sexy.

"How old are you?"

"Uh...er...uh...five," she said.

"I don't think so, hon. If you were five, your eyes and beak would be yellow, your wings all brown and your head and tail white."

"Aaah...I dye my feathers to make myself look younger."

"You should be home with your parents."

"Well, pops, I guess if you had a mate, you'd be home with her, now wouldn't you?"

The image of Leu and Aquilo cut across my field of vision like a chainsaw. The immature female flittered to another branch. An eagle from a few limbs over spoke up.

"Hey, pal, why don't you leave the ladies alone, okay?"

"And, hey, who would be making me leave the ladies alone...pal?"

"Me," the eagle said, pushing his chest out.

"You and what flock?"

Two of the Brood's bouncers pinned my wings back, dragged me outside and roughed me up.

"And stay out, pal," they said as they shoved me into a gravel bar."

"THEY MURDERED YOUR GREAT GRANDFATHER RIGHT here in the Chilkat Valley; gunned him down in front of his wife and two children."

"Yes, Grandpa."

"He was in the prime of his life, only twelve-years-old."

"Yes, Grandpa."

"It was a bad time to be an eagle back then. We call it the Massacre, the Reign of Terror. They slaughtered 100,000 of us over a 35 year span. Wiped out entire families."

"Yes, Grandpa." There was good news and bad news back then...

"There was good news and bad news back then, boy. Good news was the rivers were packed with spawned out, dead, decaying salmon. The bad news was we were all dead and decaying, too."

Grandpa chuckled and coughed up a pellet or two. I waited patiently.

"Bad news was we were all dead and decaying, too," Grandpa repeated, jettisoning another pellet across the nest.

"Yes, Grandpa."

"So," my grandfather said after a long silence, "you're having some female problems, are you?"

"Yes, Grandpa."

"And you've come by to visit your old grandfather for some sage advice. Am I correct?"

"Correct."

"Well, my boy," Grandpa said, putting an old, battered wing over mine, "I can't help you. I haven't a clue."

My bill dropped open. I tried to say something.

"You know, the killings stopped way before you were hatched... the Feds didn't always protect us...you kids take the Preserve for granted...I remember the first..."

"GET THIS THING OFF OF ME!"

Canus was wrapped up in a fish net he had dragged from the river. Fovea Joe, Clo and I slowly untangled the mess. Canus shook his feathers.

"You should stick to bread bags," I said.

"Hrmmmph," Canus said.

"6,101, 6,102, 6,103..."

"We warned you about being involved in this mating game, Hal," Fovea Joe said.

"Warned you a million times," Clo said, "...6,222, 6223..."

"Watch out for her mother, I told you," Canus said.

"Wait, fellas, I need advice on how to get her back, not on how to stay away from her."

The gang sat there, no expression, staring out at the river.

"You know," I said, "now that I think about it, have any of you ever been mated?"

"Of course I have," Fovea Joe said, "...well, not really...sort of...what's your point?"

"Yeah, what are you getting at?" Canus said. "If I wanted to be mated, females would be lined up and down the Chilkat River. It would look like the largest congregation of eagles in the world."

"Thousands," Clo said.

"Right, fellas," I said, "and I have a nest in a clear-cut to sell you."

I FLEW UP THE TSIRKU, CROSSED OVER TO THE KLEHINI River, flapped all the way down the Chilkat past Davidson and Rainbow glaciers, then across Mud Bay and back through Haines.

Then it hit me. I would build a nest. I found a tall spruce on the banks of the Tsirku near the entrance to Chilkat Lake where the sockeyes go to spawn. Crazed like a magpie, I hauled twigs, moss and debris to my building site. In three to four days I had built a nest that looked like an ad for the Forest of Dreams.

I was putting some finishing touches on the place—moss in the center, fireweed around the outside—when I heard the flap of wings above me. It was Leu.

"Good location, Hal. Nice tall tree. Serves as a superb observation post and acts as a signal to unwanted visitors. The height also provides unobstructed flight paths for us as eagles since we have a problem becoming airborne and maneuvering in dense foliage."

"I knew that," I said weakly.

We sat in silence while I nodded my head up and down.

"Hungry?" I said, looking around the nest. "I know I've got something flopping around."

"No, I'm stuffed. I stole a sockeye from a couple of Canadian eagles on my way over."

"Where's Aquilo?" I asked, the name sticking in my craw.

"Oh, Aquilo has gone back south. We had some species and genus issues."

"Hmmm."

"And I have to get back to work," Leu said, flapping her wings.

"Wait, Leu. Why don't you tuck your wings back and stay a while? We could preen a little, maybe do some light talon locking. Like old times.

What do you say?"

"Old times give me a headache, Hal."

"But these are new times."

"Not yet, Hal. I'll call you."

Leu dropped out of the nest and flapped her wings. A feather from her breast fluttered in the wind and landed on the nest. I gently picked the feather up with my bill and placed it in the center of the twigs. I sat and admired it. One, I said to myself as I started to laugh. Only 7,181 more to go.

AUTHOR'S NOTES

The Bald Eagle is of the genus Haliaeetus (hals, Greek for sea, and aetos, eagle) and the species Leucocephalus (white-headed). The sub-species of the northern Bald Eagle is Alascanus.

The fovea is a cup-like depression in the retina, home for a high concentration of sensory cells.

Between 1917 and 1952, Alaska offered a 50-cent to $2 bounty on the Bald Eagle. More than 100,000 eagles were shot and killed.

SALMON

A Revelation Story

I'VE ALWAYS BEEN AN EMOTIONAL FISH. MY FRIENDS attribute my moods to my overly sensitive lateral lines, pores that run down my body from head to tail. These pores hook up with a canal under my skin that connects with my brain, helping me sense minute disturbances and subtle movement. That's how I pick the best current, swim through murky water and maintain the tight formation of my school.

But I think my sensitivity has more to do with unresolved issues from my troubled childhood. I'm an orphan. My mother and father died when I was conceived. I lived under a half-foot of gravel in Chilkat Lake for six months before I emerged from my alevin stage to become a fry. I fought for a year with my 4000 brothers and sisters over cheap crustaceans and microscopic algae slop—green desmids, blue diatoms and blue-green dinoflagellates. I huddled in fear of swim-by killings when the Chars, a gang of crazed fish high on zooplankton, wiped out ninety of my siblings in one swallow.

Only a few good salmon, a hundred or so from each family, are fortunate enough to survive to become smolts and head out to the saltwater. I was one of the proud, brave, and I suppose, lucky. I spent my years at sea dodging fishnets and battling an ocean of food-frenzied whales, sharks and sea lions. Many times I came within a scale's length of a brutal death from cruise ship rudders. Blown off course by cross currents, I still managed to travel over 2000 miles a year. The light at the end of this long Inside Passage was, of course, the happy spawning ground.

To spawn, to reproduce, is the ultimate goal for a salmon, a reward for a hard-fought life. A return to the spawning ground is a return to where we were born. Although I have never met a salmon that has spawned, fantasies of the spawning ground, a mysterious, sensual garden of delights, have danced in my brain for the last four years. I dreamed of mating with my special love, floating around the lake all day, joking with my buddies. Not a care in the world.

And, now, here I was, at the beginning of the last leg of my odyssey, treading water in front of a sign at the mouth of the Chilkat River that read:

CHILKAT LAKE
"HOME OF THE SPAWNING SOCKEYES"
25 MILES
SWIM SAFELY.

MY BUDDIES AND I WENT DOWN TO CELEBRATE OUR
last day in saltwater at Sockeye Sushi, a bar and restaurant 100 feet below
the surface of the Lynn Canal, right near the mouth of the Chilkat River.
A banner outside the joint read, "Last Stop For Food." Inside, Fry and the
Fingerlings sang "Let's Spawn 'Til Dawn" on the jukebox.

There was Milt, who was originally from a rival school before he transferred
over to us last month when his entire graduating class was kidnapped near
Juneau and never heard from again. Milt and I hit it off right away, as if we
had known each other our entire lifecycle. Some fish mistook us for brothers
and couldn't tell us apart.

Alevin was the brain of our school, a graduate of the Migratory School
of Limnology, the study of lakes, ponds, streams and the life they contain.

Gill, on the other fin, was an airhead and a paranoid hypochondriac. He
ranted on and on about a global conspiracy to capture all of us Sockeye
and ship us off to foreign lands in cans and jars. Whatever you say, Gill.

We had covered over twenty miles that day and we were starved.
We polished off a platter of arrow worms, a bowl of bivalve larvae,
twelve orders of snails, three mixed invertebrate plates and ten Alaskan
amphipod rolls. While I squiggled over to the All-You-Can-Eat-Kelp-
Bed, the fellas started their usual arguments. Want to get a school of
salmon riled up? Ask them how we can possibly migrate thousands of
miles and still find our way back to the spot where we were born.

"What I'm trying to tell you boys," Milt said, chewing on an ostrocod,
"is that it's all smell. We've got a half million receptors per square inch up
our noses. We follow the scent, baby. It's as simple as that."

"No way, Milt," Gill said, spacing out for a minute as he watched the air
bubbles from his mouth float to the surface. "It's electricity, man. See,

as ocean currents travel across the earth's magnetic field, electricity is created and we pick up those signals with our lateral lines. Takes us home. If THEY don't get us first."

"Gill, you've got the brain of a copepod," Al said, pushing his glasses up the bridge of his pectoral fin. "Our cycle is planted deep inside, imprinted on our chromosomes. Our homing ability is an inherited response to our environment."

"Hey, Red, what do you say?" Milt said to me as I swam back from the kelp buffet with a plate piled high with Fucus, Porphyra and Nereocystis.

"I don't care how we get there," I said, sucking in a strand of Ulva, "I just want to get upstream and start spawning."

"Here, here!" the boys cheered, raising their cups of Vin du Plankton, "to spawning!"

"Listen," I said, tilting my snout toward the jukebox. King Chinook was singing a bluesy version of "Hate Being Late to Mate Your Date." We rocked back and forth, lip-synching to the song.

"YOU ARE ONE OF THE CHOSEN."

I didn't sleep well that night, flipping and flopping, jumping out of the water a few times. I dreamed of my deceased mentor, the great holy fish, the Dolly Salmon, who lived in exile underneath a kelp bed until he was tragically crushed to death by bags of garbage thrown into the ocean from a cruise ship.

I met the Dolly when I was still a smolt, not more than three or four inches long. Our currents crossed the day I had my first brush with the Sea Monster, the Humpback whale.

I've never been fond of whales. They're fat gluttons who think they're so smart. If they are so intelligent, how come they sing the same stupid song over and over again?

So, there I was, on my first day at sea, when a whale opened his mouth and started sucking in hundreds of my people, along with herring, krill and part of an oil slick. I watched from a safe distance, out of his current of death. I got steamed and swam up along side him, staring him straight in his left eye.

"Hey, fat boy," I said, "I'm not always going to be this small. The next time we meet, you're mine."

The whale gave me a smirk and went off humming his annoying tune. I whacked him on his side with my tail and took off to catch up with what was left of my school.

"Pssssst."

I swished my tail, looking behind me.

"Pssssst, down here."

I looked down and saw an old salmon peeking out from a kelp bed. I dove down to get a closer look.

"Hello, Sockeye," he said.

"Uh, hello...ah..."

"I am the Dolly Salmon. I will be your mentor."

"Hmmm...mentor. And what does that mean, exactly?" I asked, a little suspect of this old salmon of the sea.

"I will tell you things."

"Such as?"

"You are one of the chosen."

"Sounds like a fortune cookie I read last week at Swim Lo's."

"It is your fortune, Sockeye."

"Oh, yeah. Okay, thank you, I guess. What else?"

"Swim swiftly."

"Swim swiftly? Thanks for the tip, Dolly, but I have to get going."

"Sockeye?"

"Yeah?"

"To the blind, all things are sudden."

"Gotcha. Later."

I swam off, but as odd as he was, something about him stuck with me.

And now, the night before the last leg of my journey, he appeared to me in a dream.

"You are one of the chosen," he repeated from years ago. "It is your destiny and purpose."

"Whatever," I said, turning to go.

Suddenly empty bottles, tin cans and dirty napkins poured down from above, burying the Dolly Salmon.

"SPAWNING   GROUND!   SPAWNING   GROUND!
Spawning Ground!"

I awoke to the chanting rumble of thousands of salmon swarming at the starting line of the Spawn Marathon, the endurance race to the spawning ground. I joined the fellas and wiggled my way into place at the mouth of the river.

"Spawning Ground! Spawning Ground! Spawning Ground!"

I felt pressure on my tail fin.

"Hey, watch your snout, pal," I snapped at a sockeye behind me.

"Spawning Ground! Spawning Ground! Spawning Ground!"

Every salmon was pumped. Thousands of gills pulsed the water with their short, deep breaths.

The race official dropped his dorsal fin and the race was on. We pushed, wiggled and squiggled. We were still in the saltwater, but a hint of fresh water tickled my gills, flickering something primordial in my brain. I flipped my tail and jumped ahead of the fish in front of me. I felt good.

"Watch out! Net!" Al yelled. "Dive!"

Instinctively I let the air out of my swim bladder and dove to the bottom for safety, the sound waves of my captive brothers vibrating through the water as the net dragged them toward the surface. My nose banged into the silty bottom. I fluttered my tail to balance myself and to gather my wits. Al and Milt were beside me. But where was Gill?

"Who's paranoid now?" Gill hollered.

We looked up. Gill stared down at us from the netted mass of salmon, rising above us like a storm cloud. I was staring helplessly at the surface when I heard a laugh and turned to see a couple of flounder feeding on the bottom. They were smiling.

"Good luck, salmies," one flounder yelled.

"Yeah, you'll need it," said the other.

I surged toward them but Al stopped me.

"Let it go, Red, they're not worth it. They're bottom feeders."

I'D WITNESSED MANY SLAUGHTERS AND I'D LOST many friends over the years, but it never gets easier. We quickly recited the 23rd Salmon Psalm for Gill and regrouped.

We continued upstream, into the dark current. I was back in the fresh water for the first time since I was a youngster. I thought I would miss the salt, but I felt good, healthier without it. We fought the downstream current as it shoved us off our rhythm, slamming us back against the rocks lying in the river. We pulled over after a few hours to catch our breath.

"Want anything to eat?" I said, watching a gaggle of cladocerans crawl by us.

"Never thought I'd turn down a fresh water crustacean, but, no, I'm not hungry," Milt said.

"Me, neither," I said.

"You guys," Al said, "we salmon don't eat anymore once we enter the fresh water. There are a couple of other things you both should know—"

"Not now, professor," I said, anxious to push on with our pilgrimage.

We continued up the Chilkat until the last light of day faded deep behind the mountains. We stopped in an eddy and curled up for the night while Al put us to bed with a hot little story about a sexy female salmon.

"She digs a spot for her eggs in water about twelve inches deep with a surface current eighteen inches per second, slow enough so the eggs aren't washed away. The hole itself is between four to twelve inches. Then she buries the fertilized eggs in six inches of gravel. She'll lay thousands of eggs, but that's nothing compared to the female mola mola, the nine-foot-long sunfish whose giant ovaries contain 300 million eggs and—"

"Enough!" I said, fanning myself with a fin. "Is it just me or is this river heating up?"

"Must be an aquifer bubbling up around here, cause my temperature's rising," Milt said.

"Hard to get any sleep around here with stories like that, Al," I said.

"Sweet dreams, boys," Al said, chuckling.

"Thanks, Al."

I WAS IN THE MIDDLE OF A LARGE LAKEBED. THOUSANDS of salmon swam below me as I floated along the surface. There were tiny alevins, small fry, larger smolts and full-grown adults. The Dolly Salmon appeared next to me. He had a plastic ring from a six-pack container wrapped around his neck and a piece of Styrofoam stuck in his tail fin.

"That's my cousin, Coho, and my distant relative, Humpy, and Uncle Silver," I said, looking down as we scooted across the water. "Wait a minute, there's Gill. Where are we, Dolly Salmon"?

"This is the Spawned Beyond, Sockeye. Every salmon passes through here."

"I'll be here someday, I suppose."

"Someday," the Dolly said.

"But, not for awhile, I've got a lot of business to take care of, you know."

The Dolly Salmon nodded his head, smiled and said, "Sockeye—"

SOMETHING SHARP LIKE CORAL TORE AT MY SIDE AND ripped me awake.`

"Bear! Bear! Swim for your lives!" I yelled.

The bear stomped into the water, his big furry paw slapping for me again. I faked left, then shot back right. Water was splashing everywhere. Fish were flopping and flying into each other, trying to escape. Pain streaked from snout to tail as I scooted away from the bear. I stopped and looked around. Milt, his eyes the size of oyster shells, circled a pair of eyeglasses lying on the river bottom.

"Where's Al, Red? Where's Al?"

I squinted up through the murky water and saw the hairy beast on the shore, leaning into the river, Al in his claws. As the bear opened his mouth, I accelerated through the water, timed my jump and leaped into the air, biting down hard on the paw holding Al. The bear roared and reared up, but he refused to loosen his grip on my friend. I fell on the gravel bar and quickly wiggled back into the water. I swung around in time to see the bear's mouth close over Al's head.

I treaded water for a moment, my mind frozen in denial. Then I swam away in grief, memories of a shark attack that killed friends of my family flashing through my brain—another act of senseless violence against the Sockeye salmon.

"ARE YOUR TEETH GROWING LONGER, IS YOUR JAW elongating, your snout hooking, your back humping, your skin thickening and your body absorbing your scales, or are you just happy to see me?"

"Excuse me?"

"Hi, I'm Ova."

She was a pretty girl with a big belly.

"I'm Red. Big Red."

A couple of male salmon swam close to Ova, giving her the once over. I lunged and snapped at them.

"Sorrrrrry," one of them said as they headed upstream.

Ova giggled and turned a deep shade of salmon pink. Then she looked at me with concern.

"You're bleeding."

"Oh...yeah." With all that had happened I'd forgotten that the bear had cut me.

"Your operculum appears to be damaged."

"What?"

"Oh, I'm sorry," she said, "your operculum, your gill cover. I'm a crash unit nurse over at the Saturday Night Salmon Fights."

She flippered over to me and gave me a quick exam.

"It's just a scale wound," she said, "you're fine."

"So are you," I said.

She flushed a deeper shade of red and gave me a little swat with her tail.

"I think the fresh water is going to your head," she said, with a twinkle in her eye. "You don't know me well enough to talk to me like that."

"But I like to talk to you like that," I said.

"Then you should get to know me better."

"Well, how about—"

"I'll be up in Chilkat Lake," she said, spinning around to go. I watched her tail swish gently back and forth as she headed upstream.

"HELLO, DOLLY."

"Hello, Sockeye."

We were again floating above the Spawned Beyond. In the middle of the sea of salmon I saw a familiar face.

"There's Al," I said.

"Yes, Sockeye."

"Al's dead."

"In some ways, Sockeye."

"What's he waiting for in that line?"

"That's the line for the Reincarnation Debarkation Station."

"What do you get there?"

"Your reward."

"Reward? Great. He didn't even get to spawn. It better be a good reward."

"Your reward is fulfilling your destiny and purpose, Sockeye," the Dolly Salmon said as he nodded and smiled.

"Wow, I'm sure glad I'm chosen, right, Dolly"?

"Sockeye," the Dolly Salmon said, "there is something you must know—"

Suddenly, paper plates, cups, beer bottles and animal bones descended through the water, blurring my connection with the Dolly Salmon.

I DIDN'T FEEL GOOD. I WAS TIRED ALL THE TIME. I FELT like I had a chronic case of Saprolegnia Parasitica, the deadly white furry moss that is fatal to salmon. I hadn't eaten in days and I was bruised and beaten from bouncing off rocks while fighting the downstream current.

But Milt and I pushed on.

We reached the confluence of the Chilkat and Tsirku rivers and instinctively took a left and started up the Tsirku delta. The water was shallow and the current slower. The gravel rubbed my belly as I moved upstream.

"What's that?" I said.

"Sounds like music," Milt said.

We slowed down, the sound of singing echoing through the water, vibrating my lateral lines.

"Over there," Milt said, motioning with his snout.

A school of smolts on their way out to sea surfed on the downstream flow. They were young, fresh and full of promise, their whole lives in front of them. As they swam closer and looked over at us, their eyes bulged out of their sockets.

"Aaaaaaaaah! Look at those teeth! The hump on his back! No scales! Aaaaaaaah!"

I looked around. There was no one behind me. Were they talking about me? The smolts scattered off to another channel, screaming and yelling.

"How do I look?" I asked Milt.

"Uh, well, you look...great, Red," Milt said, leaning against a gravel bar, breathing heavily.

"Well, I don't see why they were so afraid of me, Milt. If your teeth get any longer you could pass for a beaver."

"I was trying to be polite, Red, but since you asked, the bigger the hump on your back gets the more you look like a killer shark."

"Hey, that's a cheap shot, Milt. The way your head is turning green doesn't exactly—"

"What are we fighting for, Red?" Milt said. "We need to conserve our energy. Look, let's take this shallow channel. It'll be easier."

I followed Milt up the thin stream, my body half out of the water. Milt picked up speed and pulled ahead of me, not noticing a sharp turn in the channel.

"Wheeeeeeee!" Milt yelled.

"Watch out, Milt, slow down!"

Milt missed the turn and beached himself on a gravel bar. He squirmed and squiggled trying to get himself back into the water.

"C'mon, Milt," I hollered, "you look silly."

"Just a second, Red," Milt said, "I'm almost there."

First I thought it was a cloud covering the sun as a shadow fell over us. But when I heard the flutter in the wind, followed by a high-pitched wail, I knew it was trouble. I watched in horror as an eagle snatched Milt in its talons and slowly struggled to drag him off the ground.

"Hey! Drop him!" I screamed at the eagle as I jumped out of the water, bouncing toward them. The eagle tried to gain momentum for lift off but I pushed out of the water and bit it on the wing. The eagle crashed and shifted Milt to its left talon, attacking my neck with its beak. Then the bird of prey sliced its right talon across my stomach, knocking me back onto the gravel bar and pinning me to the ground with its talon.

"We got a problem here?" the eagle said. "Stick around, I'll be back."

With Milt still in its grasp the eagle furiously flapped his wings. I tried to get up but the lack of water and loss of blood weakened me. I squiggled on the gravel bar while I watched my last friend fade into the sky. The cold and darkness smothered me.

"DO YOU KNOW YOUR NAME?"

"Uh, yeah...uh, Red."

"Do you know what year of your lifecycle you're in?"

"Um...fourth, no, fifth."

"Do you know where you're going?"

"Uh...why, are you lost?"

I was floating in shallow water. Ova was tending to me.

"I remember being dragged from the gravel bar. I thought it was the eagle coming back for me. I didn't have any strength to fight him. But it was you."

"Here, have some more water," Ova said, as she pulled me further into the stream. She was applying pressure to different parts of me with her fins.

"How do you feel, Red?" she said.

"Never felt better. A fish net took my friend Gill, a bear ate Al and an eagle just took off with Milt. Myself, I feel like I've been run through the turbines of a dam. Looks like a win-win to me."

"Well, you're alive. Your airway is open, your breathing is restored and your circulation is maintained. I think I've stopped the bleeding. You were in shock."

"Shock?"

"Yes, you were chilled, breathing harshly, nauseous, clammy and pale."

"And how do I look now?"

"You look...ah...ah...better. More important is how you feel."

"I wish I felt as good as you look."

Ova's body flushed an even deeper red, her head glittering with a hint of green.

"You're obviously feeling better, Red, and your bleeding has stopped. But you should rest for the night and recover your strength. I have to go. The entrance to Chilkat Lake is just around the bend. Why don't you come up and get to know me better."

She gave me a smooch with her big lips and swished away.

AFTER OVA LEFT, I FLOATED ALONE WITH MY thoughts. Here I was, just a few strokes away from my destination, the end of my journey. The Happy Spawning Grounds. Party Time.

But everyone I'd spent my life with was dead, and, by all rights, I should be dead as well. Why had I been spared?

I wondered about Ova. What part did she play in my journey? Why did she appear whenever I needed help?

Because I was one of the chosen! That's why. Now the Dolly Salmon's words made sense. I had been chosen to spawn.

And spawn I would.

Every day I would spawn in memory of my fallen brothers. I would name my first 100 sons Gill, the next 100 Al, the next 100 Milt. Every morning, while Ova and I served them fresh algae, I would tell the kids about their namesakes. They would have the father I never had. Of course, the day would come when our kids would be ready to go out to sea by themselves and we'd hope we had empowered them with enough knowledge to help them live fulfilling lives in the deep. Then Ova and I would curl up and retire in a corner of Chilkat Lake and wait for their return.

I had a big job ahead of me and, as Ova said, I needed my rest for the last of my quest. I settled into the water and let sleep lap over me.

I SWAM EFFORTLESSLY UPSTREAM, FULL OF VIGOR. THE Dolly Salmon appeared beside me.

"Oh, great holy fish," I said to him, "I've lived my whole life by instinct, gone with the flow, never questioned much. And now, as I near my home after all these years and obstacles, I feel confident about my ability to fulfill my destiny and purpose."

The Dolly Salmon nodded his head, closed his eyes and smiled.

"But I have one last question for you, Dolly."

"Yes, Sockeye?"

"What do I do with my life after I spawn, oh, great denizen of the deep?"

The Dolly Salmon nodded his head again, closed his eyes and smiled.

"You die, Sockeye."

I shook my head to get the water out of my ears.

"Excuse me?"

"It is your gift to the universe."

"Really? Don't you think the universe has enough gifts? I planned on spawning the rest of the year."

"You spawn but once, Sockeye."

"Once! After all I've been through, I spawn once!"

"It is your fortune."

"Oh, please."

"It is better to have spawned and died than to never have—"

"Tell it to the universe," I said as I curled into a semi-circle and exploded out of the kelp bed.

I WOKE UP WET AND COLD, SHAKEN AND DISTURBED.
To spawn or not to spawn. That was the question. I'd suffered the
claws and talons of outrageous fortune and I'd fought against a sea of
troubles. But no, the universe wanted more gifts. And what do you give
the universe? The answer, it seemed, was floating in the stream. You give
the universe whatever it wants.

Now I was to spawn, to die: to die, perchance...to what?

I stewed most of the morning in a stretch of slack water near the
entrance to Chilkat Lake. Revelations swirled around me like an
eddy. Of course I'd never met a salmon that had spawned. And no
wonder the support group, Salmon and Orphans, was so popular.

I watched school after school of smolts singing and playing on the
first leg of their odyssey. Who among them would be the chosen? I
watched the best of my generation drag their tired, disfigured bodies
up the river. How many of their friends had died?

As the steady torrent of young smolts rushed past me and the elders
fought their last battle, suddenly it all became clear. I was part of a
continuous cycle of young and old, birth and death. I realized how
foolish it was of me to fight the flow. I was one of the elite. I had seen the
world and lived to come home, the last surviving member of my family.

"You are one of the chosen."

The pull of instinct, faster than thought, washed over me. I burst out of
the water, my wasted body invigorated with purpose. I played the current as
if I was a smolt again. I rounded the bend into Chilkat Lake and bumped a
couple of fellow Sockeyes out of the way.

"Sorry, boys, I'm on a mission."

I scooted over the lakebed and there I was, in the Spawning Ground.

As far as I could see, red bodies and green heads frolicked together in pairs while bitter bachelors fought to break up happy couples.

"Over here, Red."

It was Ova. She was digging the perfect redd near the shore of the lake.

"You're just in time, honey," she said, giving me a big wet kiss while putting the finishing touches on the redd, testing its depth with her anal fin.

"Timing's everything," I said, admiring the green hue of her head.

I was nibbling her ear when a male Sockeye swam by and bumped us. I snapped at him, sinking my teeth into his tail.

"You want a piece of me?!" I growled at him, spitting out a chunk of his flesh. "You want a piece of me?!"

"Hey!" the male salmon said, slicing away from me while blood from his wound stained the clear water. "You've got a serious attitude there, buddy."

"Sorry about that, honey," I said, caressing one of her lateral lines with my snout, "now where were we?"

"That was cute," she said, giggling.

Ova winked at me and settled down into the redd, closed her eyes and ground her teeth. Her body shuddered and hundreds of transparent eggs began dropping into the gravel. I slid down beside her and fertilized the eggs as they piled up in the redd.

Afterwards we used our tails to lovingly tuck our eggs safely under the gravel. Then we nuzzled together.

"You know, Ova, we're two of the chosen."

"It's our fortune, Red. The Dolly Salmon told me that a long time ago."

"What?" I said, startled. "The Dolly Salmon appeared to you, too?"

"Shhh," Ova said as she put her tail over mine.

I rubbed her snout one last time. Then, feeling complete and fulfilled, I closed my eyes and let myself slip away into the late afternoon light.

MRS. CLAUS
A Bottom Line Story

I WAS BORN TO RUN A FORTUNE 500 COMPANY. AT AGE seven I owned, operated and franchised a chain of successful drive-through lemonade stands. In middle school I reengineered the cafeteria food lines to maximize playground time. As high school treasurer, I funneled "donations" through the principal's office to soften his views on independent study.

I went on to earn my MBA from a prestigious business school in the Midwest. For my master thesis I evaluated the efficiency of my own school's business department. As a result of my recommendations, four professors were denied tenure, two assistants were urged to "pursue other opportunities" and my advisor, an old friend of the family, was stripped of his pension.

Upon finishing my Workaholic in Residence Program at the local branch of the Foreclosure Bank of North America, I graduated at the top of my class. Recruiters fought over me as if I were a blue chip athlete. I chose a small-cap, high growth company with rapid multiple product introductions. Within months, with my solution-oriented instincts for problem solving, I became an invaluable member of the senior management team. However, after the first leg of my oxygen-depleting career arc, I found myself curiously unfulfilled.

I set a goal to get back on track. I hired a Chinese Feng Sui master to re-energize my office. Mr. Woo built a moat around my desk and filled it with exotic Asian goldfish. He hung crystals from my ceiling and replaced my phone ringer with a ceremonial gong. I reread the #1 bestseller, "Rationalizations Seven Successful CEOs Use to Convince Themselves They're Doing Something Worthwhile With Their Lives." I even refused to work more than 12 hours on Sundays.

Nothing helped. Was it me? Was it my job? Headhunters contacted me constantly, but I turned down lucrative offers every day. Then, one night, at 2 a.m., I turned in early. While flossing my teeth, checking my voice mail and balancing my check book, the business section fell off my lap onto the floor. I leaned out of bed and a block of letters from the page expanded in front of me:

IMMEDIATE OPENING!!!!

EFFECIENCY EXPERT AT THE NORTH POLE

SERIOUS INQUERIES ONLY

The North Pole! Now, that sounded interesting. I emailed my resume from the laptop I kept on the nightstand next to my bed. I nodded to sleep and tiptoed into dreams. I skied across the white frosting of a gigantic birthday cake with lit candles the size of pine trees. I laughed and giggled until a horn went off in the wilderness. I stomped my feet and yelled for it to stop. I woke up to the sound of my computer telling me I had a message. I reached over, turned on the light and checked my messages.

Would like to schedule an interview tomorrow night. Is midnight
okay? My driver will pick you up. Dress warm.

Ho-ho-ho

S.C.

To the amazement of the cleaning crew, I left work by eleven that night.
I rushed home and changed into my blue wool power suit; assertive
but friendly. I opened my laptop and reviewed my list of compensation
requirements—short term and long term bonus potential, transportation
allowance, 401 k, stock options, first dollar medical and dental.

My computer scheduling program beeped. There was a thud at the
door. It was midnight. I put the laptop in my briefcase, grabbed my coffee
cup and stepped onto the porch of my condo. On the sidewalk stood
eight reindeer and a shiny, red sleigh, glowing like a hot coal.

"Wow, reindeer," I said, icicles racing down my extremities.

"You think?"

"Excuse me?" I said, looking around for the source of the voice. The
reindeer in front of the pack turned to me.

"I said, 'You think?' What part of that didn't you understand, lady?"

I dropped my briefcase, coffee spilled over my shoes.

"Talking reindeer."

"We've got a smart one here, fellas."

The other reindeer chuckled and stomped their hooves into the ground.

"You must be here to pick me up?" I said foolishly.

"No, lady, we were just in the neighborhood looking for our cousin
Rudy and we thought you might be roasting him over an open fire."

The reindeer laughed, stomped and nudged each other with their
antlers. They mumbled parts of the joke: "...just in the neighborhood...
open fire...might be roasting..."

I checked my watch, straightened my suit, trying to act businesslike in
front of eight talking reindeer. I reached my hand out to the head reindeer.

"Hi, I'm—"

"Bob."

"Sorry?"

"Name's Bob, ma'am. You have a problem with that?"

"No...uh...Bob is a lovely name...for a talking reindeer."

"Bob is a lovely name for a talking, flying reindeer, lady. Let's go."

I stepped up into the sleigh and grabbed hold of the reins, a feeling of wonder sizzling my skin. The reindeer shuffled their hooves and lifted off, the momentum plastering me to the seat. We rose above the trees, the houses and the high rise office buildings. We flew north, above a quilt of clouds, the stars blinding me as if they were flashbulbs. Bob told stories while the reindeer joked and sang. I held on, the wind biting my face, spinning my hair into steel wool.

As we began our descent, the greens and reds of the Northern Lights danced in my head like a cartoon. We landed in the middle of the light show, on a snowed-in runway with a barely visible sign that read:

WELCOME TO THE NORTH POLE

SNOW FELL AROUND ME LIKE FEATHERS FROM A celestial pillow fight. I stepped out of the sleigh, took a breath and composed myself. Shoulders back, briefcase in hand, I trudged through the snow and opened the door to the complex. A voice yelled:

"You Better Watch Out!"

An avalanche of clutter buried me in darkness, a bike pedal stuck in my ribs, a basketball flattening my ear. Somewhere out there a talking doll repeated, "I'm Patty and I'm not afraid to say 'no.'"

I heard someone digging me out of my tomb. A colander of light flowed through the spokes of a wheel pressed to my face. I looked up into a wall of red.

"Are you okay?"

"You're Santa Claus!" I yelled, as if he were an amnesia patient.

He nodded and helped me up. We were standing in a warehouse the size of a cruise ship. With the inventory system of my grandfather's garage, dolls, skis, clothes and games were stacked to the ceiling.

"Be right with you," Santa said, one hand full of crumbled papers, the other searching through the debris.

"Um, you lose something?"

"Not yet. Just can't find it right now," he said, looking up and shaking the papers at me. "Checking a list, you know."

Santa began excavating a corner, tossing packages and toys behind him like a dog digging a hole. He looked at me and shrugged. He walked over to a pair of rocking horses and sat on one, motioning for me to sit on the other.

"Things are a little disorganized right now," Santa said with a flip of his chubby hand and a nervous "Ho-ho-ho."

I rocked a few times, assembling my thoughts.

"This is your fulfillment center, I take it?"

"What's that?"

"This is where you fill your orders for gifts, right, Mr. Claus?"

"Uh, right."

"What type of database do you use?" I asked, rocking back and forth on my horsy.

"Database?"

"Database. How do you keep track? I mean, some years I get some pretty weird stuff, as if my list was crossed with somebody else's."

"Well, yeah, that happens once in a while," Santa said defensively.

"How do you control your inventory?"

"I check the list twice," he said with pride.

"That doesn't do much good if you're checking the wrong list, now does it?"

"Well..."

Santa looked around the room, down at the papers in his hand.

"I'd like you to come in for a month or so and work out some of the glitches we've developed."

"A month or so?" I said, stopping my rocker. "I think you're underestimating the extent of your glitches, Mr. Claus."

"Nah, this is different than other businesses you deal with."

That's what they all say, I thought, as I reached for my laptop. Santa and I worked for an hour or two before he tired and went to bed. I stayed up and created spreadsheets and made to-do lists. Halfway through my personal brainstorming I eyed a pair of nearby rollerblades and couldn't resist the urge to lace them up. I skated around and around the warehouse floor until I collapsed, exhausted, in a heap of teddy bears, the images of reindeer dancing in my head.

"BAAAAATTER UP!"

The chatter of vowels jerked me awake. Funny looking children were jumping around me with frying pans in their hands. They tossed pancakes from one to another, singing gibberish about batter and syrup.

> Put the heat up on the griddle
> Put the batter in the middle
> And flip those babies in the air

I sat up. Wait a minute, I said to myself, looking at the bells on their pointy shoes and their goofy little hats. It's the elves!

"Hey, what's going on here?" I said.

They turned to me and froze, flipped pancakes flopping on top of their heads. The elves bounced over and introduced themselves. There was Flapjack and Griddlecake and Blintz and Chapatty and Crepe and Pfannekuchen and the Stack Brothers—One, Two and Three.

While they fed me breakfast (Swedish, German and apple pancakes) they told me their story. Raised in an orphanage run by a mean, black-balled short order cook, they were fed only pancakes. One morning, during a grease fire in the kitchen, they escaped, and with the aid of Elf-Self-Help, a temporary elf employment agency, they found work at the North Pole. They took on batter related names, became gourmet flapjack chefs and constantly sang the classic ode to the pancake, "Batter Up."

I passed on a strawberry waffle and a blueberry blintz, my urge to work overcoming my hunger.

"What time do you boys have to be at work?"

"Whenever," they shrugged.

"What are you working on today?"

"Whatever."

"Hmmm," I said as I prepared for my nine o'clock with Santa.

SANTA WAS LATE AND HIS OFFICE WAS A MESS,
stacked high with papers. I picked up a letter from the top of the pile
and read it:

Dear Santa,
I'm not happy. You used to be nice but you don't give me the stuff I ask
for anymore. Take me off your list and give my name to the Easter Bunny.
Georgia
Age 6

I read twenty more letters in the stack, all of them with the same
complaints. Santa walked in, yawning and rubbing sleep from his eyes. I
waved the letters at him.

"What happened to their gifts?"

"I don't know," he said, running his hands through his hair. "It happens
once in a while."

"Define 'once in a while,'" I said, sweeping my hands over the reams of letters.

"Well..."

"Listen, Mr. Claus, it's only February and we have time to straighten
things up around here. However, before I do anything, I need to ask your
office manager a few questions."

"Office manager?"

I SENT AN EMAIL TO MY OFFICE INFORMING THEM I was working off-site for a while. Then I began my evaluation of the work flow at the North Pole.

I sat down with the elves and had them describe their jobs to me. I asked them what their major complaints were and how we could resolve those issues. Although they mentioned shortage of raw materials, frantic, last minute production and various safety hazards in the workshop, they said they never viewed them as problems because that was the way it had always been. Bob and his crew felt the same way. Sure, there were flight delays and extended holding patterns, Bob said, but that was the price of doing business on Christmas Eve. Job satisfaction was rated high by all.

By the end of February a project scope was in place with timelines and milestones to help ease the December crunch. By March, with the elves pulling all-nighters with me, we had a complete stock inventory. In April the database was up and running, listing the gift receivers by region, age and gift request history. During May Bob and his herd and me and my stopwatch began our monthly practice runs, testing new routes and timing our deliveries.

Santa was impressed and pleased with the reorganization, but he showed little interest in learning about the business side of his operation. Not much of a head for it, he would say as he "Ho-ho-hoed" through the complex. However, I insisted upon giving him monthly slide presentations, weekly status reports and sitting him down for a daily dinner meeting where I reviewed the day's events.

I eliminated 52 rework loops by June. Everyone had a copy of "From List to Delivery," a 750 page manual I threw together for reference points. There were T-shirts and posters on the walls that proclaimed our motto:

RIGHT LIST

RIGHT GIFT

RIGHT PERSON

RIGHT TIME

On Christmas Eve I gathered Santa and the elves in the living room. I wore the red dress and black boots the elves made for me.

"I want to thank everyone for all the hard work you put in to make the new changes—"

There was a bang on the window. Bob glared at us through the window.

"Hey! Excuse me!" he yelled.

I ran to the door and opened it wide. The eight reindeer tromped into the living room, knocking over furniture with their rumps, poking the elves into the air with their antlers.

"Hey! Watch it, Bobby!" Flapjack said, rubbing his bottom.

"Welcome," I said when the commotion died down.

"Nice to be invited, ma'am."

"Now, Bob, the Delivery Team Meeting isn't for ten minutes," I said, pointing to my watch. "You would know that if you'd read today's memos."

"Must have missed that one, ma'am. I could just kick myself."

"Save your strength, Bob. Let me kick you."

The other reindeer laughed and butted antlers. I thanked everyone again, then handed out gifts—red nose warmers to the reindeer and real maple syrup to the elves. After our final checklist we were ready to hit the sleigh.

"Okay, you know the drill, let's go!"

With the precision of an Indy 500 pit crew, the elves funneled the sleigh with gifts and strapped harnesses on the reindeer. Santa jumped in the driver's seat and grabbed the reins. I sat beside him, my laptop loaded with the list database with corresponding maps in one hand, a cup of hot chocolate with marshmallows in the other. I turned to Santa.

"Ready, Mr. Claus."

"Ready," Santa said. "On Bob."

The reindeer pulled hard, jerking the sleigh forward like a railroad car. We lifted off, circled around the complex and headed south, the wind at our backs. Bob and Santa bantered back and forth, telling stories of Christmas past. We stopped at small houses and large houses, at hospitals and orphanages, wherever there were children who needed toys.

I kept an eye on the time as I checked the list twice. I fed the crew Reindeer Power Enhancement Bars when their energy levels dipped. I was all business and this was my watch. When we hit Haines, Alaska, one of our last stops, a heat surged through me. The snow covered rooftops and the Christmas trees in the windows made me clap my hands and hug myself in delight. It was Christmas Eve night and I was riding along in Santa's sleigh!

"Ho-ho-ho, Merry Christmas," Santa said as we landed on the air strip back at the Pole.

"Merry Christmas to you, Mr. Claus," I said, checking my watch and making one last entry in my computer.

We sat silently in the sleigh, toasted by the glow of giving, watching the falling snow cleanse the night. I looked over at Santa and for the first time, I thought—he's kind of cute.

"ARE YOU SEEING ANYONE?"

"Sort of."

"I thought so. You don't call for almost a year. A year! I have to call your office to find out you've quit your high paying, high profile job and moved to Northern Poland."

"No, mother, not Northern—"

"So, what does he do?"

"He works with underprivileged children and—"

"There's no money in that."

"It's non-profit, mother."

"There is plenty of money in non-profit, dear. A CEO can make a bundle—bonus, compensation, padded expense accounts. You just have to keep it quiet."

"Please, mother—"

"I'll plan on you two coming for Christmas this year."

"That's not a good time for us, Mother."

"You owe me that much, don't you think, for all I've done for you?"

"Well, okay, but we can only stay for a second."

I NEVER CONSIDERED THE CHANCE OF ROMANCE in any work environment, let alone the North Pole. After our first Christmas success, Santa wanted to take a few weeks off, but I insisted we get back to work bright and early on December 26th. There was much to do and I stressed to Santa that he had much to learn about running a successful company.

As we continued to work together, I felt the heat of proximity. Something was melting at the North Pole and it wasn't from global warming. Whether it was his beard tickling my arm as I handed him a graph or when I would squeeze by his soft, round belly on my way to the printer, there was the tingle of love at the North Pole.

I denied the feelings at first. He was my boss, for goodness sake. How many articles in women's magazines had I read about this very peril? Then there was the age issue. I didn't know how old Santa was, but he was at least as old as my mother.

I could tell Santa had similar feelings for me. I caught him staring at me while I prepared spreadsheets and work tasks. He would look away, turn redder than usual, and give a self-conscious "Ho-ho-ho."

We took walks out in the snow while I taught him about process mapping, reengineering and rework loops. One day I slipped on the ice and he caught me and held me tight.

"Are you okay?"

"Yes, thank you, Mr. Claus," I said, resting my head on his chest.

"Call me Santa," he said.

We stood there, the wind frisking us, Santa's heart pounding in my ear. Goodness radiated from somewhere deep inside his girth, a spot I had never found within myself. Where I came from people gave in order to control others, their apparent generosity really a chit to be cashed in at an opportune time. But Santa had a purity of heart that flowed into me like a blood transfusion.

We married a few months later during a blizzard in front of the workshop. Bob, who became an ordained minister through a number he found in the back of Reindeer Journal, performed the ceremony. The reindeer sang and danced while the elves threw dollar pancakes.

We didn't have time for a honeymoon, I told Santa, but maybe next year. There was too much to be done. My proactive production plan was a week behind schedule, the number of flight delays was unacceptable and the stopover time ratio made me toss and turn all night.

The next year, during the first week of December, right on schedule, we had a baby boy, Sammy. Sandy came along a year later. I told Santa it was time for me to take one step back from the business and for him to take one step forward. With confidence in my system, I stayed home with the kids on Christmas Eve.

And life was good.

For his fourth birthday Santa gave Sammy a miniature chimney with real soot. At five, he gave our son a sleigh cycle with voice activated stuffed reindeer. By six, Sammy was putting on weight and "Ho-ho-hoing" around the house.

As a child, Sandy rode on her daddy's shoulders while Santa went about preparing for Christmas. "List" was one of the first words she learned after "Mama," "Dada," and "Bob." The elves workshop was my own little day care center for her. Sandy loved sitting with Flapjack at his workbench, laughing and clapping, eating hotcakes and singing along to "Batter Up."

Yes, life was good.

"DAD, CAN I DRIVE THE SLEIGH THIS YEAR?"

"Not this year, Sammy. Maybe next year."

"You say that every year."

"Do I? Well, not this Christmas. Maybe next year."

"Then can we finally go to Hawaii for a vacation?"

"This year is too busy. Maybe next year."

"I'm going to be 12 next week. All I ask for every Christmas is for you to take me to Hawaii."

"We don't give you great gifts?"

"Yeah, everything but what I want."

"So why don't you and Bob go? He'd love it."

"Bob? Dad, I want to go with you. That's the point."

"Maybe next year."

"Let's talk about this after dinner," I said.

"Not tonight, dear," Santa said. "I have to work late at the shop."

Sammy, head down, poked his food with his fork, staring at his pasta as if it were a pile of worms.

THINGS WERE CHANGING AT THE NORTH POLE. AT first I thought it was all for the good. Santa took my advice and became active in the nuts and bolts of the company. He drilled me on basic business theories and subscribed to 25 business magazines, from Business Week to Downsizer to Loopholes Monthly. He read every column in the Wall Street Journal except the editorials.

Driven by his new knowledge, he realized the department store process arc from Halloween to Christmas Day was too small a window of opportunity. Santa hit the road year round promoting his image on talk shows, at Pro-Mythological golf tournaments and summer camps for future street corner Santas. He sponsored a professional wrestling extravaganza—the Battle of the Department Store Santas.

It all appeared to be working so well. The number of letters from disgruntled children dwindled. Santa was more popular than ever, immortalized in new songs and hit movies, buried in an avalanche of fan mail. He was voted "Sexiest Man Alive" for an unprecedented three years in a row.

But the more time he spent with the world, the less time he spent with his family. Sammy, now in his teens, withdrew, watched his weight and went on weeklong juice fasts. Sandy rebelled, turning her room into a shambles, refusing to use the index system I designed for her closet. She immersed herself in the teachings of obscure pagan religions.

Then the layoffs began.

"LET ME GET THIS STRAIGHT, FAT MAN. YOU'RE shuffling me and the crew out to the back 40 for some kind of spacecraft?"

"Hovercraft, Bob."

"Oh, hovercraft. Well, excuse me and my big ignorant rump."

Bob and Santa never argued. I could see and hear them through the window as they stood outside the complex, the falling snow bleaching them into the backdrop.

"Let me ask you this, Santa baby. Have me and my crew ever missed any deliveries?"

"No, of course not."

"Have we ever been late on our rounds?"

"No."

"So, everything's fine. Well, it must be time to send the boys to the sausage factory."

"Early retirement, Bob."

"Early retirement. Well, it's too early to retire. We love our job. And you're not the only star around here. They write songs about us, too. 'Here comes Santa and his hovercraft' is not what I would call a catchy hook."

"Bob, this move is for technological advancement. I think you'll see this is best for the company."

"Best for the company? How many years have we broken our backs hauling your fat butt all over the world? And you're telling me what's best for the company doesn't include us?"

"You're not looking at the big picture, Bob."

"Oh, yeah, well I've got a big picture for you right here, fat man."

Bob turned around and wiggled his rump in Santa's face, then stomped through the snow to the stable. Yes, things were changing at the North Pole.

"WE'RE LIMITING OUR RESOURCE ALLOCATION TO strengthen our core business."

"Wow, cool, Santa."

I was standing outside the office. I recognized Flapjack's voice through the door.

"As a valued member of our transition team, we would like to offer you an incentive to relocate."

"Relocate?"

"Yes."

"Leave the North Pole?"

"Yes, Flapjack. Next year we will be outsourcing our production to some cost-saving labor markets. We need you to relocate as a consultant."

"But this is my home, Santa. All my friends are here. I don't know anybody outside of here."

"This is a terrific vertical move for you, Flapjack."

"But I'm happy right here. I don't want to go."

"There's no longer a job for you here. There is a job for you down there."

The door opened and Flapjack, his head down, shuffled by me. I stepped inside the office. Santa beamed and opened his arms.

"Isn't this great, honey?" he said. "I do have a knack for this side of the business."

Santa kissed and hugged me tight, squeezing the breath out of me.

"I owe it all to you, honey."

ON HIS 18TH BIRTHDAY SAMMY MOVED AWAY FROM THE North Pole. He was now a thin, gaunt young man, withdrawn and sullen. He seldom laughed. He bummed a ride off of Bob, who was more than happy to fly him to Hawaii where Sammy went into retail.

Four months later, Sandy, distraught over the relocation of Flapjack, ran away from home. She joined a cult that neither exchanged gifts nor celebrated holidays. Her sect believed that rodents were reincarnated holymen and Sandy founded The Creatures Are Stirring, a solidarity group for mice. She changed her birthday to February 2, Groundhog Day.

Santa minimized the impact of their departures.

"They're kids, honey, it's a phase. Look, I think I've figured out a drop shipment system that will cut some fat off our payroll."

The next few Christmas Eves I spent alone, sitting in my rocking chair, the house smothered in silence. Santa was out in the hovercraft with its Global Positioning System and automatic list checker. How did it come to this, I thought, as my head nodded up and down, in and out of sleep, memory tugging at me like a puppet string. After all my work, how did I end up all alone, with no friends or family, just like I was before I came to the North Pole?

Then, on one more lonely Christmas Eve, with a draft biting my ankles and my rocker creaking a sad tune, Griddlecake ran into the room.

"Mrs. Claus, Flapjack has disappeared."

I sat up, shook my head, leaned forward.

"I just received a call from the factory down south," Griddlecake said. "Flapjack didn't show up for work today, Mrs. Claus. He wouldn't do that on the busiest day of the year."

My mind was clearing, my head buzzing, a jar full of bees.

"What are we going to do, Mrs. Claus? He must be in trouble."

I reached over and hugged Griddlecake.

"I'll go find him and bring him home."

I stood up, moving with instinct, vision and purpose. I went to the closet and put on my old red dress. It must have shrunk, I thought as I bent over and pulled on my black boots. I made my way across to the reindeer stable and opened the door. A wave of snow surfed in on the wind. "Bob," I said, "let's ride."

THE SLEIGH WAS RUSTY, THE PAINT FADED. BOB AND his crew had grown thick around the middle and the elves had to expand the harness straps to make them fit.

"Where we headed, Mrs. C?" Bob asked, pumped for action.

"South, Bob."

"Let's do it boys."

We took off into a headwind and fought our way across the latitudes. We landed somewhere in the Yukon. Bob and his crew huffed and puffed.

"Is there a problem?" I asked.

"Uh...(cough, heave)...nothing, Mrs. C."

"You boys a little winded?"

"Us...(hack)...no way. Never felt better. Right, fellas?"

The other seven reindeer nodded as they coughed and sputtered.

"...you got that right...top of our game...feel great..."

After a brief rest we continued south to the state of Washington. Bob stopped for a break on Mount Rainier, and then we flew over Mount Saint Helens, down the Columbia River and up the Willamette River to Northeast Portland. I found the address I wanted on Tenth Street.

I walked up the stairs and knocked on the door. An army of tiny feet tap danced away as a pair of big feet marched toward me. A curtain parted, a doorknob turned. Sandy poked her head through the opening.

"Mom. What are you doing here?"

"I need your help. Let me in."

Sandy didn't move, her face scrunched up as if focusing on a complicated math equation.

"Sandy Claus, open this door. NOW!" I said, stomping my boot on the porch.

Startled, she stepped back and I walked past her. An altar with cheese and treadmills stood in the center of the candle-lit living room. Mice scampered back and forth.

"This place is a mess. Grab your coat. I need your help."

"I can't leave, Mom," Sandy said in a hushed tone. "I have a duty and responsibility here. Do you know who these mice are? They're reincarnated holymen, and I'm their sworn protector."

Sandy pointed around the room.

"This is Krishna, and Buddha, Mohammed, this is Moses, and gee, Gandhi is around here somewhere."

"That's very nice, dear, but we have to go."

"Mom—"

"Sandy, get your coat. I need you. You owe me that much."

"Owe you, Mom? Is that what giving is all about? The more you give, the more you're owed?"

My mother's voice echoed in my head and a sharp pain from childhood burrowed into my stomach. I closed my eyes and focused on my mission.

"We have to go, NOW!" I said, stomping my boot on the floor again. I felt a squish under my heel, heard a pop like a walnut in a nutcracker. Sandy and I looked down at my boot. She bent over.

"Oh, no, Mom, it's Gandhi. He doesn't look good."

"I'm sorry, honey, but he'll be back...someday."

She held the mouse in her hands like a chalice.

"Honey, Flapjack is missing from his post."

Sandy looked up at me, her eyes wide, the elf's name a Pavlovian trigger to her childhood. She dropped the dead mouse on the floor.

"Missing? What does that mean?"

"I don't know. That's why we have to hurry. NOW!"

"Watch where you step, Mom! I'm coming."

I held the door open for Sandy while I watched Moses and Mohammed spinning on their treadmills.

WHILE SANDY HUGGED THE REINDEER, I JUMPED BACK in the driver's seat and we headed west, the wind raking us with needles of rain. Bob and his herd slid into a groove, singing and joking like old times. The weather cleared when we turned south over the Pacific Ocean.

Stars twinkled and whales breeched as we approached the island of Maui. We landed on the main street of Paia, the last address I had for Sammy. The stores lining the street stood wrapped in Christmas decorations and draped in banners of holiday cheer. My son's shop sat at the end of the block, its black-striped candy cane neon sign blinking: THE ANTI-CHRISTMAS STORE. When we neared his storefront he stormed out the front door and chased away a group of Christmas carolers.

"And Merry Christmas to you," I said.

He whirled around like a gunfighter. Recognition softened his face.

"Mom...Sandy...Bob?"

"How's business, son?"

"Oh, a little slow," he said defensively, sounding like his father.

"Imagine that."

"Very funny, Mom," he said.

"Flapjack is missing, son, and you can help us find him."

"Why should I? So you can send him back to that awful factory?"

"We're taking him back to the North Pole, where he belongs. Where we all belong."

"I don't belong there."

"We don't have time for this, son. Come with us."

"I can't help you, Mom."

Bob reared up on his hind legs, pulling at the harness like a bull in a stall.

"Don't you talk to your mother like that, boy! Let me at him!"

Bob dragged the rest of the team toward the building and pinned Sammy against the wall with his antlers.

"Get your butt in this sleigh right now or I will stick these antlers in your behind and drag you with us. What'll be, Sammy Boy?"

"Okay, Bob, okay, but I'm not staying at the North Pole."

"Who would want you around with that attitude? Now, get in the sleigh."

Sammy climbed into the back of the sleigh and slumped into the corner. I looked over at Bob, but he looked away.

SANDY TOLD US TO FLY TO CALIFORNIA. IN HIS LETTERS, she said, Flapjack told her Venice Beach was the only place he seemed to fit in. We zoomed across the ocean and landed near the Venice Pier.

"Where do we start?" I asked Sandy.

"He said he sings in a bar around here," Sandy said.

"That should be easy to find," Bob snorted, "he only knows one song."

We walked down the strand, Sammy sulking behind us. We showed Flapjack's picture to street corner Santas as they roller-skated by, but they only shook their beards. We turned down a street lined with restaurants and bars. Through the wall of holiday music flowing from the building we heard the strains of an old familiar song. Sandy grabbed my arm as a raucous chorus of "Batter Up" roared from inside a biker bar across the street.

"Look!" Sandy yelled.

Flapjack, with bells on his slippers and his little elf hat on his head, stumbled out of the bar, through a row of motorcycles and dropped to his knees over a sewer drain.

"Flapjack!" we all said as we ran to him.

"Mrs. C., Sandy, Sammy...Oh, I don't feel so good."

Flapjack put his head down, recycling a meal into the gutter. I leaned over him, the smell of liquor sucking the air out of my lungs.

"Flapjack, you're drunk. You don't drink."

"But I'm unhappy, Mrs. C."

"Getting drunk doesn't help, Flapjack."

"It doesn't? But that's what unhappy people do down here. Boy, am I sick."

"Come on, Flapjack, we're taking you home."

"I don't have a home anymore."

"Yes, you do. We're taking you back to the North Pole."

"I'll be good, I swear I will."

"You were never bad, Flapjack."

"I must have done something terrible to make Santa send me away, Mrs. C."

I picked Flapjack up and hugged him, my mind muddled with emotions. A huge, bearded man dressed in leather walked out of the bar and started up his motorcycle. He noticed Flapjack and pointed his finger at us.

"Hey, little dude, the pancake song rocks."

SANDY HELD FLAPJACK'S HEAD OVER THE SIDE OF THE sleigh as Bob guided us north over the old delivery route we had honed so many years before. Above Haines, the necklace of lights rimming the small boat harbor triggered memories of my first Christmas run with Santa and the dull ache of the past swept over me. Flapjack perked up, as if from a cattle prod.

"Down there!" he said. "It's Santa!"

Santa lay sprawled in the snow, gifts scattered around him like confetti. The hovercraft sat smashed into a building in the middle of the parade grounds. We landed and the four of us rushed to Santa's side.

"Santa, are you okay?" I said, my heart exploding. "What happened?"

"Oh, my leg," he moaned, dazed by shock. "Darn machine doesn't listen to me like Bob did."

Santa chuckled a weak "Ho-ho-ho."

"It's not broken, honey," I said after I squeezed my hands down his leg. I checked my watch. "The deliveries are way behind schedule. Let's use the sleigh."

The kids and Flapjack gathered the gifts and loaded the sleigh. We huffed, puffed and grunted to get Santa on his feet but when I watched him hobble I knew he was in no shape to chimney hop. Santa tried to slide into the driver's seat, but Sammy stopped him.

"Get in the back, Dad."

"I'm driving, Sammy."

"You've already wrecked one vehicle. Get in the back and relax. I'm driving."

"This is my sleigh and I'm driving."

"Not now you're not. But..." Sammy said, pausing for effect, "maybe next year."

Santa stared at our son, frowned, then nodded in revelation. We helped him into the back seat and I sat beside him, keeping his leg elevated. When Sammy grabbed the reins, Flapjack turned to me.

"We don't have a list, Mrs. C."

"Oh, yes, we do," I said, reaching under the seat for my laptop and turning it on. I squinted at the blur on the screen, feeling through my pockets for my reading glasses. Sandy snatched the computer from my lap.

"I'll handle this, Mom. You take care of Dad."

"On Bob," Sammy said as we taxied along the snow and then up into the night sky. I sat back, Santa's head in my lap, and watched our children work. Sandy checked the list while Flapjack refilled the sack between stops. Sammy, with the fervor of a firefighter, slid up and down the chimneys. With speed, enthusiasm and teamwork they finished ahead of schedule.

"This is Big Red to base," Sandy said into the radio. "Do you copy?"

"This is base," Griddlecake's voice scratched through the air.

"We've got Flapjack and we're coming home."

"That boy can drive a sleigh," Bob said as we landed back at the Pole, the Northern Lights blazing like a Mardi Gras party. Griddlecake and the gang raced out of the complex, hugging Flapjack and Sandy and freeing the reindeer. Blintz and Chapatty ran back inside to get a stretcher for Santa while the reindeer danced and slapped antlers in celebration of their trip.

The purity and joy of the moment bathed me in light. I looked down at Santa and took his hand. He turned to Sammy who was standing in front of the sleigh, staring at the complex.

"Nice job, son," Santa said.

Sammy nodded and walked away. I squeezed Santa's hand and stroked his head.

"Let's talk, Santa," I said.

An hour later we gathered for breakfast in the dining room. Bob had everyone laughing. The big reindeer was telling jokes, doing impressions, reliving the night's highlights. Pancakes sat on the table, piled high like stacks of poker chips. I tapped on a gallon jug of maple syrup.

"I want to welcome Flapjack back to the North Pole," I said.

Applause, hooting, tossing of pancakes.

"And I also want to thank Sandy and Sammy for visiting us."

More applause, stomping of hooves, slapping of antlers.

"Santa and I have been talking and we've made a few decisions. First, if Bob and the crew agree, Santa wants them back next year as his delivery team."

"Early retirement for the hovercraft!" Bob said, raising a hoof in the air.

"Second, we are returning to our centralized production system, which means we need you back, Flapjack."

"Yes!" the elves said, exploding from their seats like sports fans.

While I watched the reindeer dance on tables and listened to the elves sing "Batter Up," I thought about my life at the North Pole. What a success I had been at efficiency, but what a failure I was at effectiveness. How many times had I towed the bottom line of low cost production when the real bottom line was celebrating right before me?

"Mom, are you okay?"

I shook my head and turned toward Sandy, who was swing dancing with Bob.

"Pardon me, honey?"

"I said, 'Are you okay?' You're staring."

"Oh, I'm fine, sweetheart."

Sandy rushed over and hugged me, squeezing me tight.

"I love you, Mom."

Bob stepped up and gave me a wet, slobbering kiss, his breath stinging my eyes. I mopped my cheek with my sleeve.

"I love you, too, Mrs. C."

The elves and the other reindeer rushed to me, kissing and hugging me as if I'd scored a winning soccer goal. Sammy fought through the crowd and whispered in my ear.

"Merry Christmas, Mom," he said.

My throat was tight, my skin massaged by electricity. I grabbed Santa's hand so I wouldn't float away. I made a goal to get back on track, but this plan came from my heart, not my head. What was good for me would be good for our family, and what was good for our family would be good for our company, and what was good for our company would be good for the world.

Now that's a bottom line I could live with.

More Titles by Tom Lang: